The Forever Girl

ALEXANDER
McCALL
SMITH

The Forever Girl

PANTHEON BOOKS,
NEW YORK

THIS BOOK IS FOR
NEIL AND JUDY SWAN

This is a work of fiction. Names, characters, places, and incidents either are the product of the author's imagination or are used fictitiously. Any resemblance to actual persons, living or dead, events, or locales is entirely coincidental.

 Published in the United States by Pantheon Books, a division of Random House LLC, New York, and in Canada by Alfred A. Knopf Canada, a division of Random House of Canada Limited, Toronto, Penguin Random House companies. Originally published in Great Britain by Polygon Books, an imprint of Birlinn Limited, Edinburgh, in 2014.

Pantheon Books and colophon are registered trademarks of Random House LLC.

Library of Congress Cataloging-in-Publication Data
McCall Smith, Alexander, [date]
The forever girl / Alexander McCall Smith.
pages cm
ISBN 978-0-307-90825-4 (hardback). ISBN 978-0-307-90826-1 (eBook).
1. Families—Fiction. I. Title.
PR6063.C326F65 2014 823'.914—dc23 2013038944

www.pantheonbooks.com
www.alexandermccallsmith.com

Jacket art by William Low
Jacket lettering by Iain McIntosh

Printed in the United States of America
First United States Edition
2 4 6 8 9 7 5 3 1

Part One

I

I have often wondered about the proposition that for each of us there is one great love in our lives, and one only. Even if that is not true – and experience tells most of us it is not – there are those, in legend at least, who believe there is only one person in this world whom they will ever love with all their heart. Tristan persisted in his love of Isolde in spite of everything; Orpheus would not have risked the Underworld, one imagines, for anyone but Eurydice. Such stories are touching, but the cynic might be forgiven for saying: yes, but what if the person you love does not reciprocate? What if Isolde had found somebody she preferred to Tristan, or Eurydice had been indifferent to Orpheus?

The wise thing to do in cases of unreturned affection is to look elsewhere – you cannot force another to love you – and to choose somebody else. In matters of the heart, though, as in all human affairs, few of us behave in a sensible way. We can do without love, of course, and claim it does not really play a major part in our lives. We may do that, but we still hope. Indifferent to all the evidence, hope has a way of surviving every discouragement, every setback or reversal; hope sustains us, enables us to believe we will find the person we have wanted all along.

Sometimes, of course, that is exactly what happens.

This story started when the two people involved were children. It began on a small island in the Caribbean, continued in Scotland, and in Australia, and came to a head in Singapore. It took place over sixteen years, beginning as one of those intense friendships of childhood and becoming, in time, something quite different. This is the story of that passion. It is a love story, and like most love stories it involves more than just two people, for every love has within it the echoes of other loves. Our story is often our parents' story, told again, and with less variation than we might like to think. The mistakes, as often as not, are exactly the same mistakes our parents made, as human mistakes so regularly are.

The Caribbean island in question is an unusual place. Grand Cayman is still a British territory, by choice of its people rather than by imposition, one of the odd corners that survive from the monstrous shadow that Victoria cast over more than half the world. Today it is very much in the sphere of American influence – Florida is only a few hundred miles away, and the cruise ships that drop anchor off George Town usually fly the flag of the United States, or are American ships under some other flag of convenience. But the sort of money that the Cayman Islands attract comes from nowhere; has no nationality, no characteristic smell.

Grand Cayman is not much to look at, either on the map, where it is a pin-prick in the expanse of blue to the south of Cuba and the west of Jamaica, or in reality, where it is a coral-reefed island barely twenty miles long and a couple of miles in width. With smallness come some advantages, amongst them a degree of immunity to the hurricanes that roar through the Caribbean each year. Jamaica is a large and tempting target for these winds, and is hit quite regularly. There is no justice in the storms that flatten the houses of the poor in places like Kingston or Port Antonio, wood and tin constructions so much more vulnerable than the bricks and mortar of the better-off. Grand Cayman, being relatively minuscule, is usually missed, although every few decades the trajectory of a hurricane takes it straight across the island. Because there are no natural salients, much of the land is inundated by the resultant storm surge. People may lose their every possession to the wind – cars, fences, furniture and fridges, animals too, can all be swept out to sea and never seen again; boats end up in trees; palm trees bend double and are broken with as much ease as one might snap a pencil or the stem of a garden plant.

Grand Cayman is not fertile. The soil, white and sandy, is not much use for growing crops, and indeed the land, if left to its own devices, would quickly revert to mangrove swamp. Yet people have occupied the island for several centuries, and scratched a living there. The original inhabitants were turtle-hunters. They were later joined by various pirates and wanderers for whom a life far away from the prying eye of officialdom was attractive. There were fishermen, too, as this was long before over-fishing was an issue, and the reef brought abundant marine life.

Then, in the second half of the twentieth century, it occurred to a small group of people that Grand Cayman could become an off-shore financial centre. As a British territory it was stable, relatively incorrupt (by the standards of Central America and the shakier parts of the Caribbean), and its banks would enjoy the tutelage of the City of London. Unlike some other states that might have nursed similar ambitions, Grand Cayman was an entirely safe place to store money.

"Sort out the mosquitoes," they said. "Build a longer runway. The money will flow in. You'll see. Cayman will take off." Cayman, rather than the Cayman Islands, is what people who live there call the place – an affectionate shortening, with the emphasis on the *man* rather than the *cay*.

Banks and investors agreed, and George Town became the home of a large expatriate community, a few who came as tax exiles, but most of them hard-working and conscientious accountants or trust managers. The locals watched with mixed feelings. They were reluctant to give up their quiet and rather sleepy way of life but found it difficult to resist the prosperity the new arrivals brought. And they liked, too, the high prices they could get for their previously worthless acres. A tiny white-board home by the sea, nothing special, could now be sold for a price that could keep one in comfort for the rest of one's life. For most, the temptation was just too great; an easy life was now within grasp for many Caymanians, as Jamaicans could be brought in to do the manual labour, to serve in the restaurants frequented by the visitors from the cruise ships, to look after the bankers' children. A privileged few were given *status*, as they called it, and were allowed to live permanently on the islands, these being the ones who were really needed, or, in some cases, who knew the right people – the people who could ease the passage of their residence petitions. Others had to return to the places from which they came, which were usually poorer, more dangerous, and more tormented by mosquitoes.

Most children do not choose their own name, but she did. She was born Sally, and was called that as a baby, but at about the age of four, having heard the name in a story, she chose to be called Clover. At first her parents treated this indulgently, believing that after a day or two of being Clover she would revert to being Sally. Children got strange notions into their heads; her mother had read somewhere of a child who had decided for almost a complete week that he was a dog and had insisted on being fed from a bowl on the floor. But Clover refused to go back to being Sally, and the name stuck.

Clover's father, David, was an accountant who had been born and brought up in Scotland. After university he had started his professional training in London, in the offices of one of the large international accountancy firms. He was particularly able – he saw figures as if they were a landscape, instinctively understanding their topography – and this led to his being marked out as a high flier. In his first year after qualification, he was offered a spell of six months in the firm's office in New York, an opportunity he seized enthusiastically. He joined a squash club and it was there, in the course of a mixed tournament, that he met the woman he was to marry.

This woman was called Amanda. Her parents were both psychiatrists, who ran a joint practice on the Upper East Side. Amanda invited David back to her parents' apartment after she had been seeing him for a month. They liked him, but she could tell that they were anxious about her seeing somebody who might take her away from New York. She was an only child, and she was the centre of their world. This young man, this accountant, was likely to be sent back to London, would want to take Amanda with him, and they would be left in New York. They put a brave face on it and said nothing about their fears; shortly before David's six months were up, though, Amanda told her parents that they wanted to become engaged. Her mother wept at the news, although in private.

The internal machinations of the accounting firm came to the rescue. Rather than returning to London, David was to be sent to Grand Cayman, where the firm was expanding its office. This was only three hours' flight from New York – through Miami – and would therefore be less of a separation. Amanda's parents were mollified.

They left New York and settled into a temporary apartment in George Town, arranged for them by the firm. A few months later they found a new house near an inlet called Smith's Cove, not much more than a mile from town. They moved in a week or two before their wedding, which took place in a small church round the corner. They chose this church because it was the closest one to them. It was largely frequented by Jamaicans, who provided an ebullient choir for the occasion, greatly impressing the friends who had travelled down from New York for the ceremony.

Fourteen months later, Clover was born. Amanda sent a photograph to her mother in New York: *Here's your lovely grandchild. Look at her eyes. Just look at them. She's so beautiful – already! At two days!*

"Fond parents," said Amanda's father.

His wife studied the photograph. "No," she said. "She's right."

"Five days ago," he mused. "Born on a Thursday."

"Has far to go …"

He frowned. "Far to go?"

She explained. "The song. You remember it … Wednesday's child is full of woe; Thursday's child has far to go …"

"That doesn't mean anything much."

She shrugged; she had always felt that her husband lacked imagination; so many men did, she thought. "Perhaps that she'll have to travel far to get what she wants. Travel far – or wait a long time, maybe."

He laughed at the idea of paying any attention to such things. "You'll be talking about her star sign next. Superstitious behaviour. I have to deal with that all the time with my patients."

"I don't take it seriously," she said. "You're too literal. These things are fun – that's all."

He smiled at her. "Sometimes."

"Sometimes what?"

"Sometimes fun. Sometimes not."

2

The new parents employed a Jamaican nurse for their child. There was plenty of money for something like this – there is no income tax on Grand Cayman and the salaries are generous. David was already having the prospect of a partnership within three or four years dangled in front of him, something that would have taken at least a decade elsewhere. On the island there was nothing much to spend money on, and employing domestic staff at least mopped up some of the cash. In fact, they were both slightly embarrassed by the amount of money they had. As a Scot, David was frugal in his instincts and disliked the flaunting of wealth; Amanda shared this. She had come from a milieu where displays of wealth were not unusual, but she had never felt comfortable about that. It struck her that by employing this Jamaican woman they would be recycling money that would otherwise simply sit in an account somewhere.

More seasoned residents of the island laughed at this. "Of course you have staff – why not? Half the year it's too hot to do anything yourself, anyway. Don't think twice about it."

Their advertisement in the *Cayman Compass* drew two replies. One was from a Honduran woman who scowled through the interview, which did not last long.

"Resentment," confided David. "That's the way it goes. What are we in her eyes? Rich. Privileged. Maybe we won't find anybody …"

"Can we blame her?"

David shrugged. "Probably not. But can you have somebody who hates you in the house?"

The following day they interviewed a Jamaican woman called

Margaret. She asked a few questions about the job and then looked about the room. "I don't see no baby," she said. "I want to see the baby."

They took her into the room where Clover was lying asleep in her cot. The air conditioner was whirring, but there was that characteristic smell of a nursery – that drowsy, milky smell of an infant.

"Lord, just look at her!" said Margaret. "The little angel."

She stepped forward and bent over the cot. The child, now aware of her presence, struggled up through layers of sleep to open her eyes.

"Little darling!" exclaimed Margaret, reaching forward to pick her up.

"She's still sleepy," said Amanda. "Maybe ..."

But Margaret had her in her arms now and was planting kisses on her brow. David glanced at Amanda, who smiled weakly.

He turned to Margaret. "When can you start?"

"Right now," she said. "I start right now."

They had not asked Margaret anything about her circumstances at the interview – such as it was – and it was only a few days later that she told them about herself.

"I was born in Port Antonio," she said. "My mother worked in a hotel, and she worked hard, hard; always working, I tell you. Always. There were four of us – me, my brother and two sisters. My brother's legs didn't work too well and he started to get mixed up with people who dealt in drugs and he went the way they all go. My older sister was twenty then. She worked in an office in town – a good job, and she did it well because she had learned shorthand and everything and never forgot anything. Then one day she just didn't come home. No letter, no message, no nothing, and we sat there and wondered what to think. Nobody saw her, nobody heard from her – just nothing. Then they found her three days later. She was run over, thrown off the road into the bush, I tell you, and the person who did it just drive off – just drive off like that – and say nothing. How can a person do something like that to another person – run over them like they were a dog or something? I think of her every day, I can't help it – every day and wonder why the Lord let that happen. I know he has his reasons, but sometimes it's hard for us to work out what they are.

"Then somebody said to me that I could come to Cayman with her. This woman she was a sort of aunt to me, and she arranged it with some people at the church, she did. I came over and met my husband, who's Caymanian, one hundred per cent. He is a very good man who fixes government fridges. He says that I don't have to work, but I say that I don't want to sit in the house all day and wait for him to come back from fixing fridges. So that's why I've taken this job, you see. That's why."

Amanda listened to this and thought about how suffering could be compressed into a few simple words: *Then one day she just didn't come home* ... But so could happiness: *a good man who fixes fridges* ...

There was a second child, Billy, who arrived after a complicated pregnancy. Amanda went to Miami on the last day the airline would let her fly, and then stayed until they induced labour. Margaret came with David and Clover to pick her up at the airport. She covered the new infant with kisses, just as she had done with Clover.

"He's going to be very strong," she said. "You can tell it straight away with a boy child, you know. You look at him and you say: this one is going to be very strong and handsome."

Amanda laughed. "Surely you can't. Not yet. You can hope for that, but you can't tell."

Margaret shook her head. "But I can. I can always tell."

She was full of such information. She could predict when a storm was coming. "You watch the birds, you see. The birds – they know because they feel it in their feathers. So you watch them – they tell you when a storm is on the way. Every time." And she could tell whether a fish was infected with ciguatera by a simple test she had learned from Jamaicans who claimed it never let them down. "You have to watch those reef fish," she explained. "If they have the illness and you eat them then you get really sick. But you know who can tell whether the fish is sick? Ants. You put the fish down on the ground and you watch the ants. If the fish is clean, they're all over it – if it's got ciguatera, then they walk all the way round that fish, just like this, on their toes – they won't touch it, those ants: they know. They've got sensitive noses. You try it. You'll see."

Amanda said to David: "It could have been very different for Margaret."

"What could?"

"Life. Everything. If she had had the chance of an education."

He was silent. "It's not too late. She could go to night school. There are courses."

Amanda thought this was unlikely. "She works here all day. And then there's Eddie to look after, and those dogs they have."

"It's her life. That's what she wants."

She did not think so. "Do you think people actually want their lives? Or do you think they just accept them? They take the life they're given, I think. Or most of them do."

He had been looking at a sheaf of papers – figures, of course – and he put them aside. "We *are* getting philosophical, aren't we?"

They were sitting outside, by the pool. The water reflected the sky, a shimmer of light blue. She said: "Well, these things are important. Otherwise ..."

"Yes?"

"Otherwise we go through life not really knowing what we want, or what we mean. That's not enough."

"No?"

She realised that she had never talked to him about these things, and now that they were doing so, she suddenly saw that he had nothing to say about such questions. It was an extraordinary moment, and one that later she would identify as the precise point at which she fell out of love with him.

He picked up his papers. A paper clip that had been keeping them together had slipped out of position, and now he manoeuvred it back. "Margaret?" he said.

"What about her?"

"Will she have children of her own?"

She did not answer him at first, and he shot her an interested glance.

"No?" he said. "Has she spoken to you?"

She had, having done so one afternoon, but only after extracting a promise that she would tell nobody. There had been shame, and tears. Two ectopic pregnancies had put paid to her hopes of a family. One of them had almost killed her, such had been the loss of blood. The other had been detected earlier and had been quietly dealt with.

He pressed her to answer. "Well?"

"Yes. I said I wouldn't discuss it."

"Even with me?"

She looked at him. The thought of what she had just felt – the sudden and unexpected insight that had come to her – appalled her. It was just as a loss of faith must be for a priest; that moment when he realises that he no longer believes in God and that everything he has done up to that point – his whole life, really – has been based on something that is not there; the loss, the waste of time, the self-denial, now all for nothing. Was this what happened in a marriage? She had been fond of him – she had imagined that she had loved him – but now, quite suddenly and without any provoking incident, it was as if he were a stranger to her – a familiar stranger, yes, but a stranger nonetheless.

She closed her eyes. She had suddenly seen him as an outsider might see him – as a tall, well-built man who was used to having everything his way, because people who looked like him often had that experience. But he might also be seen as a rather unexciting man, a man of habit, interested in figures and money and not much else. She felt dizzy at the thought of … of what? Years of emptiness ahead? Clover was eight now, and Billy was four. Fifteen years?

She answered his question. "I promised her I wouldn't mention it to anyone, but I assume that she didn't intend you not to know."

He agreed. "People think that spouses know everything. And they usually do, don't they? People don't keep things from their spouse."

She thought there might have been a note of criticism in what he said, even of reproach, but he was smiling at her. And she was asking herself at that moment whether she would ever sleep with another man, while staying with David. If she would, then who would it be?

"No," she said. "I mean yes. I mean they don't. She probably thinks you know."

He tucked the papers into a folder. "Poor woman. She loves kids so much and she can't … Unfair, isn't it?"

There was an old sea-grape tree beside the pool and a breeze, cool from the sea, was making the leaves move; just a little. She noticed the shadow of the leaves on the ground shifting, and then returning to where it was before. George Collins. If anyone, it would be with him.

She felt a surge of self-disgust, and found herself blushing. She turned away lest he should notice, but he was getting up from his reclining chair and had begun to walk over towards the pool.

"I'm going to have a dip," he said. "It's getting uncomfortable. I hate this heat."

He took off his shirt; he was already wearing swimming trunks. He slipped out of his sandals and plunged into the pool. The splash of the water was as in that Hockney painting, she thought; as white against the blue, as surprised and as sudden as that.

3

George and Alice Collins had little to do with the rest of the expatriates. This was not because they were stand-offish or thought themselves a cut above the others – it was more a case of having different interests. He was a doctor, but unlike most doctors on the island he was not interested in building up a lucrative private practice. He ran a clinic that was mostly used by Jamaicans and Hondurans who had no, or very little, insurance and were not eligible for the government scheme. He was also something of a naturalist and had published a check-list of Caribbean flora and a small book on the ecology of the reef. His wife, Alice, was an artist whose watercolours of Cayman plants had been used on a set of the island's postage stamps. They were polite enough to the money people when they met them on social occasions – inevitably, in a small community, everybody eventually encounters everybody else – but they did not really like them. They had a particular distaste for hedge fund managers whom George regarded as little better than licensed gamblers. These hedge fund managers would probably not have cared about that assessment had they noticed it, which they did not. Money obscured everything else for them: the heat, the sea, the economic life of ordinary people. They did not care about the disapproval of others: wealth, and a lot of it, can be a powerful protector against the resentment of others. Alice shared George's view of hedge fund managers, but her dislikes were even broader: she had a low opinion of just about everybody on the island, with the exception of one or two acquaintances, of whom Amanda was one: the locals for being lazy and materialistic, the expatriates for being energetic and materialistic, and the rest for being uninterested in anything that interested her. She did not want to be there; she wanted to be in London or New York, or even Sydney – where there were art galleries and conversations, and things happened; instead of which, she said, I am here, on this strip of coral in the middle of nowhere with these people I don't really like. It was a mistake, she told herself, ever to come to the Caribbean in the first place. She had been attracted to it by family associations and by the sunsets; but you could not live on either of these, she decided, not if you had ambitions of any sort. *I shall die without ever having a proper exhibition – one that counts – of my work. Nobody will remember me.*

The Collins house was about half a mile away from David and Amanda's house, and reached by a short section of unpaved track. It could be glimpsed from the road that joined George Town to Bodden Town, but only just: George's enthusiasm for the native plants of the Caribbean had resulted in a rioting shrubbery that concealed most of the house from view. Inside the house the style was not so much the *faux* Caribbean style that was popular in many other expatriate homes, but real island décor. George had met Alice in Barbados, where he had gone for a medical conference when he was working in the hospital on Grand Cayman. He had invited her to visit him in the Caymans, and she had done so. They had become engaged and shortly afterwards she left Barbados to join him in George Town, where they had set up their first home together. Much of their furniture came from a plantation house that had belonged to an aunt of hers who had lived there for thirty years and built up a collection of old pieces. Alice was Australian; she had gone to visit the aunt after she had finished her training as a teacher in Melbourne, and had stayed longer than she intended. The aunt, who had been childless, had been delighted to discover a niece whose company she enjoyed. She had persuaded her to stay and had arranged a job for her in a local school. Two years later, though, she had died of a heart attack and had left the house and all its contents to Alice. These had included a slave bell, of which Alice was ashamed, that was stored out of sight in a cupboard. She had almost thrown it away, consigning that reminder of the hated past to oblivion, but had realised that we cannot rid ourselves so easily of the wrongs our ancestors wrought.

They had one son, a boy, who was a month older than Clover. He was called James, after George's own father, who had been a professor of medicine in one of the London teaching hospitals. Alice and Amanda had met when they were pregnant, when they both attended a class run in a school hall in George Town by a natural childbirth enthusiast. Amanda already knew that she was not a candidate for a natural delivery, but she listened with interest to accounts of birthing pools and other alternatives, knowing, of course, that what lay ahead for her was the sterile glare of a specialist obstetric unit in Miami.

Friendships forged at such classes, like those made by parents waiting at the school gate, can last, and Alice and Amanda continued to see one another after the birth of their children. George had a small sailing boat, and had once or twice taken David out in it, although David did not like swells – he had a propensity to sea-sickness – and they did not go far. From time to time Amanda and Alice played singles against one another at the tennis club, but it was often too hot for that unless one got up early and played as dawn came up over the island.

It was not a very close friendship, but it did mean that Clover and James knew of one another's existence from the time that each of them first began to be aware of other children. And in due course, they had both been enrolled at the small school, the Cayman Prep, favoured by expatriate families. The intake that year was an unusually large one, and so they were not in the same class, but if for any reason Amanda or Alice could not collect her child at the end of the school day, a ride home with the other parent was guaranteed. Or sometimes Margaret, who drove a rust-coloured jeep that had seen better days, would collect both of them and treat them, to their great delight, to an illicit ice-cream on the way home.

Boys often play more readily with other boys, but James was different. He was happy in the company of other boys, but he seemed to be equally content to play with girls, and in particular with Clover. He found her undemanding even if she followed him about the house, watching him with wide eyes, ready to do his bidding in whatever new game he devised for them. When they had just turned nine, David, who fancied himself as a carpenter, made them a tree-house, supported between two palm trees in the back garden and reached by a rope ladder tied at one end to the base of the tree-house and at the other to two pegs driven into the ground. They spent hours in this leafy hide-out, picnicking on sandwiches or looking out of a telescope that James had carted up the rope ladder. It was a powerful instrument, originally bought by David when he thought he might take up amateur astronomy, but never really used. The stars, he found out, were too far away to be of any real interest, and once you had looked at the moon and its craters there was little else to see.

But James found that with the telescope pointed out of the side window of the tree-house, he could see into the windows of nearby houses across the generously sized yards and gardens. Palm trees and sprays of bougainvillea could get in the way, obscuring the view in some directions, but there was still plenty to look at. He found a small notebook and drew columns in it headed *House*, *People*, and *Things Seen*.

"Why?" asked Clover, as he showed her this notebook and its first few entries.

"Because we need to keep watch," he said. "There might be spies, you know. We'd see them from up here."

She nodded. "And if we saw them? What then?"

"We'll have the evidence," he said, pointing to the notebook. "We could show it to the police, and then they could arrest them and shoot them."

Clover looked doubtful. "They don't shoot people in Cayman," she said. "Not even the Governor is allowed to shoot people."

"They're allowed to shoot spies," James countered.

She adjusted the telescope so that it was pointing out of the window and then she leaned forward to peer through it.

"I can see into the Arthur house," she said. "There's a man standing in the kitchen talking on the telephone."

"I'll note that down," said James. "He could be a spy."

"He isn't. It's Mr Arthur – Teddy's father."

"Spies often pretend to be ordinary people," said James. "Even Teddy might not know that his father's a spy."

She wanted to please him and so she kept the records assiduously. The Arthur family was watched closely, even if no real evidence of spying was obtained. They talked on the telephone a lot, however, and that could be suspicious.

"Spies speak on the telephone to headquarters," James explained. "They're always on the phone."

She had no interest in spies and their doings; the games she preferred involved re-enacted domesticity, or arranging shells in patterns, or writing plays that would then be performed, in costume, for family and neighbours – including the Arthurs, if they could be prised away from their spying activities. He went along with all this, to an extent, because he was fair-minded and understood that boys had to do the things that girls wanted occasionally, if girls were to do the things that boys wanted.

Their friendship survived battles over little things – arguments and spats that led to telephone calls of apology or the occasional note *I hate you so much*, always rescinded by a note the next morning saying *I don't really hate you – not really. Sorry.*

"She's your girlfriend, isn't she?" taunted one of James's classmates, a boy called Tom Ebanks, whose father was a notoriously corrupt businessman.

"No. She's just a friend."

Tom Ebanks smirked. "She lets you kiss her? You put your tongue in her mouth – like this – and wiggle it all around?"

"I told you: she's my friend."

"You're going to make her pregnant? You know what that is? You know how to do that?"

He lashed out at the other boy, and cut him above his right eye. There was blood, and there were threats from Tom Ebanks's friends, but it put a stop to the talk. He did not care if they thought she was his girlfriend. There was nothing wrong with having a girlfriend, not that that was what she was anyway. She was just like any of the boys, really – a friend. She had always been there; it was as simple as that; she was a sister, of a sort, although had she been his real sister he would not have got on so well with her, he thought: he knew boys, quite a few of them, who ignored their sisters or found them irritating. He liked Clover, and told her that. "You're my best friend, you know. Or at least I think you are."

She had responded warmly. "And you're mine too."

They looked at one another and held each other's gaze until he turned away and talked about something else.

4

Amanda was surprised. The fact that she had fallen out of love with David seemed to make little difference to her day-to-day life. That would not have been the case, she told herself, if affection had been transformed into something stronger, into actual antipathy. But she could not dislike David, who was a kind and equably tempered man. It was not his fault; he had done nothing to bring this about – it had simply happened. She knew women who disliked their husbands, who went so far as to say that they found them unbearable. There was a woman at the tennis club, Vanessa, who was like that; she had drunk too much at the Big Tennis Party, as they called their annual reception for new members, and had spoken indiscreetly to Amanda.

"I just can't stand him, you know," she had said. "I find him physically repulsive – actually repulsive. Can you imagine what that's like? Can you? When he puts his hands on me?"

Amanda had looked away. She wanted to say that you should never talk about the marriage bed, but she could not find the words. *That's private* would have done, of course, but it sounded so disapproving.

"I'll tell you," went on Vanessa, sipping at her gin and tonic, and lowering her voice. "I have to close my eyes and imagine that I'm with somebody else. It's the only way." She paused. "Have you ever done that?"

The other woman was looking at Amanda with interest, as if the question she had asked was entirely innocuous – an enquiry as to whether one had ever read a particular book.

Amanda shook her head. But I have, she thought.

"That's the only way I can bear to sleep with him," Vanessa

said. "I decide who it's going to be and then I think of him." She paused. "You'd be surprised to find out some of the men I've slept with. In my mind, of course. I've been *very* socially successful."

Amanda looked up at the sky. It was evening, and they were standing outside; most of the guests were on the patio. The sky was clear; white stars against dark velvet. "Have you thought of leaving him?"

Vanessa laughed. "Look at these people." She gestured to the other guests. One saw the gesture and waved; Vanessa smiled back. "Every one of the women – I can't speak for the men – but every one of those women would probably leave their husbands if it weren't for one thing."

"I don't think …"

"No, I'm telling you. It's true." The gin and tonic was almost finished now; just ice was left. "Money. It's money that keeps them. It's always been like that."

"Not any more, surely. Women have options now. Careers. You don't have to stay with a man you can't stand."

"No," said Vanessa. "You're wrong. You have to stay, because you can't do otherwise. What does this tennis club cost? What does it cost to buy a house here? Two million dollars for something vaguely habitable. Where do women get that money when it's men who've got the jobs?" She looked to Amanda for an answer. "Well?"

"It's not that bad."

"No, it *is* bad. It's very bad."

The conversation had left her feeling depressed, because of its sheer hopelessness. She wondered if Vanessa was at a further point on a road upon which she herself had now embarked. If that were true, she decided, she would leave well before she reached that stage. And she could: there were her parents back in New York – she could go back to them right now and they would accept her. She could take the children, and bring them up as Americans rather than as typical expatriate children living in a place where they did not belong and where they would never be sure exactly who they were. There were plenty of children like that in places like Grand Cayman or Dubai and all those other cities where expatriates led their detached, privileged lives, knowing that their hosts merely tolerated them, never loved them or accepted them.

But then she thought: she had no difficulty living with David. She did not dislike him; he did not annoy her in the way he ate his breakfast cereal or in the things he said. He could be amusing; he could say witty things that brought what she thought of as guilt-free laughter – there was never a victim in any of his stories. He did not embarrass her with philistine comments or reactionary views, as another friend's husband did. And she thought, too, that as well as there being no reason to leave, there was a very good reason to stay, and that was so that the children could have two parents. If the cost of that would be her remaining with a man she did not love, then that was not a great price to pay.

"That poor woman," said Margaret one morning. "She's going to lose a leg."

"What woman?" asked Amanda. Margaret was one of those people who made the assumption that you knew all their friends and acquaintances.

They were standing in the kitchen, where Margaret was cooking one of her Jamaican stews. The stew was bubbling on the cooker, giving off a rich, earthy smell.

"She works in that house on the corner. The big one. She's worked there a long time, but they don't treat her right."

The story could be assembled through the asking of the right questions, but it could take time.

"Who doesn't treat her right? Her employers?"

"Yes, the people in that house. They make her work all the time and then she gets sick and they say it's got nothing to do with them. She twists her leg at their place, you see, and they still say it's got nothing to do with them. Some people say nothing is to do with them – nothing at all. At their own place too."

"I see ..."

"So now the leg is fixed by that useless doctor. He kills more people than he saves, that one. The Honduran one. All those Honduras people go to him when they get sick because he says he was a big man back in Honduras and they believe him. You know how they are. They believe things you and I would laugh at – the Hondurans believe them. They cross themselves and so on, and believe all the lies that people tell them. No questions asked."

She elicited the story slowly. A Honduran maid – a woman in her early fifties – had slipped at the poolside in the house of a wealthy expatriate couple. They were French tax exiles, easily able to afford for their maid to see a reputable doctor, but had washed their hands of the matter. They had warned her about wet patches at the edge of the pool, and now she had injured herself. It was her fault, not theirs.

The maid had consulted a cheap Honduran doctor who was not licensed to practise in the Cayman Islands, but who did so nonetheless in the back of his shipping chandlery. Now infection had set in in the bone and progressed to the point that the public hospital was offering an amputation. There was an ulcer, too, that needed dressing.

The leg could be saved, Margaret said, but it would be expensive. "You could ask Dr Collins," she said. "He's a good man. He could do something."

"Has he seen her?" Amanda asked.

Margaret shook her head. "She's too frightened to go and see him. Money, you see. Doctors charge a lot of money just for you to sit in their waiting room."

"He isn't like that."

"No, so they say. But this woman is too frightened to go."

There was an expectant silence.

"All right," said Amanda. "I'll take her."

It was not onerous. And she realised that she wanted to see him. She had never been into his clinic – the run-down building past the shops at South Sound – but she had seen the badly painted sign that said *Dr Collins, Patient's at Back*. She knew that he was not responsible for the apostrophe; that was the fault of the sign-writer, and she knew, too, that it remained there because the doctor was too tactful to have it corrected. The sign-writer was one of his patients and always asked him, with pride, if he was happy with his work. "Of course I am, Wallis," the doctor said. "I wouldn't change a word of it." That had been told her by Alice.

Margaret arranged for her to pick up the Honduran woman, Bella. She did so one evening, waiting at the end of the drive while the maid, who was using crutches, limped towards her.

"My leg's bad," she said, as she got into the car. "Swollen. Bad inside. I'm sorry. It smells bad too. I can't help that."

She caught her breath. There was an odour – slightly sweet,

but sinister too; the smell of physical corruption, of infection. She wondered how this could go untreated in a place of expensive cars and air conditioning. But it did, of course; illness and infection survived in the interstices even where there was money and the things that money bought. All they needed was human flesh, oxygen, and indifference; or hardness of heart, perhaps.

She reached out and put a hand on the maid's forearm. "I don't mind. I can't even notice it."

The maid looked at her. "You're very kind."

Amanda thought: am I? Or would anybody do this; surely anybody would?

She drove carefully. The road from the town centre was busy, and the traffic was slow in the late afternoon heat. She tried to make conversation, but Bella seemed to be unwilling to speak, and they completed the journey in silence.

The clinic was simple. In a waiting room furnished with plastic chairs, a woman sat at a desk with several grey filing cabinets behind her. There was a notice-board on which government circulars about immunisation had been pinned untidily. A slow-turning ceiling fan disturbed the air sufficiently to flutter the end of the larger circulars. There was a low table with ancient magazines stacked on it – old copies of the *National Geographic* and, curiously, a magazine called *Majesty* that specialised in articles about the British royal family. A younger member of that family looked out from the cover. *Exclusive*, claimed a caption to the picture. *We tell you what he really feels about history and duty.*

Amanda spoke to the woman at the desk. She had phoned her earlier on and made the appointment, and this had been followed by a conversation with George; now there was a form to be filled in. She offered this to Bella, who recoiled from it, out of ancient, instinctive habit. And that must be how you felt if you had always been at the bottom of the heap, thought Amanda. Every form, every manifestation of authority, came from above, was a potential threat.

"I'll fill it in for her," she said, glancing at the receptionist to forestall any objection.

But there was none. "That's fine," said the woman. "As long as we have her name and date of birth."

They sat on adjoining chairs. She smiled at Bella. "It'll be all right."

"They said at the hospital ..."

She stopped her. "Never mind what they said. We'll see what Dr Collins says. All right?"

Bella nodded miserably. Then she seemed to brighten. "You've got those two children, M'am."

"Not M'am. Amanda."

"Same as me. Two. Boy and a girl. You have that Clover? I've seen her. Pretty girl."

"Thank you. Yours?"

"They're with their grandmother in Puerto Cortes. In Honduras."

"You must miss them."

"Yes. Every day. Specially now."

A consequence of the expatriate life, Amanda thought or of another variety of it.

The door behind the receptionist's desk opened. A woman came out – a young woman, tall, with the light-olive complexion of some of the Cayman Islanders. She turned and shook the doctor's hand before walking out, eyes averted from Amanda and Bella.

"Mrs Rosales?"

He nodded to Amanda; they had spoken on the phone about Bella when he had agreed to see her.

Bella looked anxiously at Amanda. "You must come too."

Amanda caught George's eye. "If she wants you in, that's fine," he said. "That's all right, Mrs Rosales. She can come in with you."

They went into the doctor's office. The receptionist had preceded them and was fitting a fresh white sheet to the examination couch. Amanda felt what she always felt in such places: the accoutrements reminded her of mortality. The couch, the indignity of the stirrups, the smell of antiseptic, the gleam of medical instruments: all of these underlined the seriousness of our plight. Human life, individually and collectively, hung by a biological thread.

Bella lay on the couch, wincing as she stretched out her damaged leg. Amanda stood back. She wanted to look away, but found her gaze drawn back to the sight of George removing the dressing. His touch looked gentle; he stopped for a moment when Bella gave a grimace of pain.

"I'm not surprised," he said. "This is very nasty."

The wound made by the ulcer was yellow. She had not expected that. She had expected red.

He probed gently with an instrument. She noticed the watch he was wearing, a square watch of a sort the advertisers claimed as *thirties retro*. She noticed that the belt he was wearing had been incorrectly threaded, missing a loop at the back. She thought of him dressing for work in the morning; dressing for his encounters with his patients, dressing for whatever the day brought him – the breaking of bad news, the stories of physical discomfort and pain; while David dressed for his meetings, his daily stint in the engine room of money. She looked at the back of his neck; at his shoulders.

Suddenly Bella reached out a hand towards her. She had been on the other side of the room, only a few feet away, but crossed over immediately and took the extended hand. She saw that there were tears in the Honduran woman's eyes.

George turned away from Bella and addressed Amanda. "She needs proper hospital treatment. Intravenous antibiotics at the very least. There might need to be some surgical excision of tissue. They'll need to get the infection under control."

She whispered. "There's no insurance. They won't send her off-island."

He shook his head. "There are some good people in Kingston. Medical missionaries from Florida. They have a first-class surgeon who knows all about these infections. I've used them before. If we can get her to them." He looked down at Bella and laid his hand on hers, the hand being held by Amanda. The three of them were holding hands now.

"I'll pay the fare. It isn't much."

"Good. That's nice of you. They'll take care of the rest."

He let go of Bella's hand and turned to the receptionist. "Can you put on a clean dressing, please, Annie?"

He drew Amanda aside. "Why has this been allowed to get to this point? Was there nobody?"

She shook her head. "The employers washed their hands of it. You probably know them. That French couple on the corner."

He raised his eyes. "They're very wealthy."

"Of course they are."

He sighed. "You said that it happened at work? In the house?"

"She slipped at work."

He asked whether she couldn't get a lawyer. "There are enough of them. This place is crawling with lawyers."

"They work for the banks."

"Of course. They work for the banks."

After the dressing had been changed, George helped Bella off the couch. He explained that he would try to make an appointment for her to see somebody tomorrow who would make arrangements for her to go to a hospital in Jamaica. Bella said nothing, but nodded her assent.

"A drink?" said George, as he showed Amanda out.

She felt her heart leap. "Why not? After I've taken Mrs Rosales home."

"Yes. The Grand Old House?" he suggested. "An hour's time? Six-thirty?"

"I haven't been there for ages."

The Grand Old House was a restaurant and bar on the shore near Smith's Cove. At night you could sit out at the front and watch the lights of boats on the water. The staff tipped food into a circle of light they created in the water and large grey fish swam in to snap up the morsels in the shallows.

She thought about the invitation as she drove home. She should call David, perhaps, and tell him, and something would have to be done about the children. They were with Margaret, at her house, and they could stay there, perhaps, until she came home. Margaret fed them pizzas and other unhealthy foods; they loved eating there.

No, she would not call David. He had said he was likely to be delayed at the office because somebody had come in from London and there was an important meeting about one of the trusts they administered. He might not be back until ten, or even later.

Back at the house, after dropping off Bella, she had a quick swim in the pool to cool off. Then she washed her hair and chose something that she could wear to the Grand Old House. She chose it with care; with the fingers of excitement already tapping at the door, insistent, unmistakable.

5

They had decided to investigate more closely what was happening at the Arthur house. The onset of cooler weather in December meant that Mr Arthur, who normally worked in an air-conditioned study, had opened his windows. The house was built in the West Indian style – both Mr Arthur and his wife came from Barbados – and had wide doors and windows under the broad sloping eaves of a veranda. If the windows of Mr Arthur's study were closed to allow the air conditioners to function, then they could not see what was going on within, even with the telescope. But with the windows open and a light switched on inside, then they were afforded a perfect view of Mr Arthur, framed by the window, at work at his desk.

"What does he do?" asked James. "He just sits there and phones. Is it all spying?"

"Teddy says that he sells ships. I asked him, and that's what he says his father does."

James looked doubtful. "Where are all the ships? In his yard?"

She agreed that it was an unlikely story. "That's probably what he's told Teddy," she said. "Because he'll be ashamed to tell his own son he's a spy. Spies don't like their family to know."

"Yes," said James. "You can't trust your own family not to tell other people."

One afternoon, they saw a man come into the study. Clover was at the telescope, but yielded her place to James. "Look," she said. "Somebody's come to see him."

James crouched at the telescope.

"What's happening now?" she asked.

"There's a piece of paper," said James. "Mr Arthur is giving it to the man. The man's handing it back to him."

"And now?"

He hesitated. "Now he's ... Look. You just look. He's burning it. He's set fire to the paper."

She resumed her place at the telescope. The instrument had shifted, but a small movement brought it back to focus on the lighted window, and she saw a man's hand holding a piece of blackened paper, then dropping it.

"Burning the evidence," she said.

"The codes," James said. "Burning the codes."

They stared at each other in silence, awed by the importance of what they had just seen.

"We're going to have to do something," James said at last.

"Such as?"

She waited for his reply.

"I think we need more evidence," he said. "We need to take photographs."

She asked how they would do that.

"We go and see Teddy. Then we take photographs while we're there."

"Teddy doesn't like us," she pointed out. "He'll wonder why we're there."

That was not an insurmountable problem in James's view. They would make overtures to Teddy – they would invite him to their tree-house, even ask him to join in their counter-espionage activities.

"But it's his own dad," objected Clover. "He's not going to like that."

"We start off by watching our own parents," he said. "That'll show him we're not just picking on him. We'll say that we have to watch everybody – with no exception. We'll say that his dad is probably innocent, but we need to prove that he's innocent."

"That'll work," she said.

He took the leadership in these matters. It was her tree-house and her telescope, but he was the leader in these games. It had never been discussed, but that was the way that things were ordered. And this was to be the case always; she would always be the one in waiting, the one hoping for recognition, for some sign from him.

She looked at him; something quite different had crossed her mind. "Have you ever heard of blood brothers?"

The question did not seem to interest him. He shrugged.

"Well, have you?" she pressed.

"Maybe. It's stupid."

She frowned. "I don't think it's stupid. You mix your blood. That makes you blood brothers. Lots of people do it."

He shook his head. He was still avoiding her gaze. "They don't." He paused. "Name one person who's done it. Name them."

"Lance Bodden. He's a blood brother with Lucas Jones. He told me. He said they both cut themselves and then put the blood together. In the palm of their hands. He said there was lots of blood."

"You can get things from that," he said. "You get the other guy's germs. There are lots of germs in blood. It's full of germs, especially if you're Lucas Jones. He's dirty."

She did not think there was much of a risk. "Blood's clean. It's spit that's full of germs. You don't mix your spit."

"I wouldn't be a blood brother anyway," he said. "Not me."

She hesitated. "We could be blood brothers – you and me."

Now he looked at her incredulously. "You're joking."

"No, I'm not. We could be blood brothers. Not with lots of blood – just a little. We could use a pin – pins don't hurt as much as knives."

This was greeted with a laugh. "But you're a girl, Clover. We can't be brothers. You have to be a boy to be brothers."

She blushed. "Girls and boys are not all that different."

He shook his head. "They are."

Her disappointment showed. "They can be friends. Best friends even."

He rose to his feet. "I have to go. Sorry."

"Because of what I said? Because you don't want to be blood brothers?"

"Not that. I've got to go home – that's all."

He began to climb down the ladder. From above she watched him. She liked the shape of his head. She liked his hair, which was dark blond and a bit bristly up at the top. Boys' hair seemed different, but she could not put her finger on the reason why it seemed different. Could you tell if it was just a single hair you were looking at? Could you tell under a microscope?

He reached the bottom of the ladder and looked up at her. He smiled. She loved his smile too. She loved the way his cheeks dimpled when he smiled. She loved him. It was a strange feeling – a feeling of anticipation, of excitement. It started in her stomach, she thought, and then worked its way up. She slipped her hand under her T-shirt and felt her heart. You fell in love in your heart, she had heard, but she was not sure how you could tell. Could you feel your pulse and count it? Was that how you knew?

Teddy was keen.

"Yes," he said. "I've often thought that people round here are hiding something."

"There you are," said James. "So what we have to do is just make sure that everybody round us is okay. We check up on them first, and then we move on to other people. We'll find out soon enough who's a spy and who isn't."

"Good idea," said Teddy. He looked puzzled. "How do you do it?"

"You watch," Clover explained. "Spies give themselves away eventually. You note where they go. You have to keep records, you see. And you take photographs. I've got a camera."

"Me too," said Teddy. "For my last birthday. It has this lens that makes things closer …"

"Zoom lens," said James knowingly. "Good."

"And then we can load them onto the computer and print them," said Teddy. "I know how to do that."

"We can begin with your dad," said James casually. "Just for practice."

Teddy shook his head. "No. Why begin with him? Why not begin with yours?"

James glanced at Clover.

"All right," she said. "We don't have to start with your dad, Teddy. We can start with mine. Or even my mum. My dad's out at the office most of the time. We can start with my mum."

"Doing what?" asked Teddy.

Clover put a finger to her lips in a gesture of complicity. "Observation."

6

He was there when she reached the bar, which is the way she wanted it to be. If she had arrived at the Grand Old House first then she would have had to sit there, in public, looking awkward. George Town was still an intimate, village-like place – at least for those who lived there – and somebody might have come up to her, some friend or acquaintance, and asked her where David was. This way at least she could avoid that, although she realised that this meeting might not be as discreet as she might wish. People talked; a few months previously at a tennis club social she had herself commented on seeing a friend with another man. It could have been innocent, of course, and probably was, but she had spoken to somebody about it. Not that she had much time for gossip, but when there was so little else to talk about ... And in due course she, and everybody else who had speculated on the break-up of that marriage, had been proved right.

She should have said no. She could have said that she had to get back to the children – they had always provided a complete excuse for turning down unwanted invitations. Or she could have suggested that he called at the house for a drink later on, and she could then have telephoned David asking him whether he could get back in time because George Collins was dropping in. And David would have told her to explain to George about his meeting and that would have been her off the hook – able to entertain another man at the house in complete propriety. But she did not do this, and now here she was at the Grand Old House meeting him without the knowledge of her husband.

She tried to suppress her misgivings. Men and women could be friends these days without threatening their marriages. Men and women worked together, collaborated on projects, served on committees with one another. Young people even shared rooms together when they travelled, without a whiff of sex. It was natural – and healthy. It was absurd to suggest that people should somehow keep one another at arm's length in all other contexts simply because their partners might see such friends as a threat. The days of closed, possessive marriages were over; women were no longer their husbands' chattels, to be guarded jealously against others.

That was a rationalisation, though, and she was honest enough to admit it to herself. She wanted to see George Collins because he interested her – it was as simple as that. She thought, with shame, of how different it would have been if it were David she was meeting for a drink; she would have felt nothing. Now something had awakened within her – she had almost forgotten what it was like, but now she knew once more.

He was sitting some distance away from the bar, at a table overlooking the sea. When he saw her come in, he simply nodded, although he rose to his feet as she approached the table. He smiled at her as she sat down.

"It's been a hellish day," he said. "And alcohol helps. I know it shouldn't, but it does."

She made a gesture of acceptance. "I'm sure you don't overdo it. But I suppose, being a doctor …"

He completed the sentence. "Makes no difference. None at all. Doctors are as weak as the rest of humanity. The only difference is that we know how all the parts work, and we know what the odds are." He paused. "Or I used to know them. You'd be surprised at how much the average doctor has forgotten."

She laughed. Talking to him was pleasant – so easy. "But

everybody forgets what they learned. I learned a lot about art when I was a student. I could rattle off the names of painters and knew how they influenced one another. Nowadays, I've forgotten everybody's dates."

He went off to order her a drink at the bar. While he was away she looked around the room, as naturally as she could. There was nobody she knew. She relaxed.

They raised their glasses to one another.

"Thank you," he said. "Thanks for coming at virtually no notice. I thought that you'd have the children to look after."

"They're with the maid. They love going to her house. She spoils them."

He nodded. "Jamaican?"

"Yes."

"They love children. They ..." He stopped himself. "Or does that sound patronising?"

She thought it did not. "It's true. It's not patronising in the slightest. Complimentary, I'd have thought. Italians love children too."

"Yes," he said. "Yes, but ... white people can't really say anything about black people, can they? Because of the past. Because of the fact that we stole so much from them. Their freedom. Their lives. Everything."

"You didn't. I didn't."

He looked into his glass. "Our grandparents did."

"I thought it was a bit before that. How long do people have to say sorry?"

He thought for a few moments before answering. "A bit longer, I'd say." He paused. "After all, what colour are the people living in the large houses and what colour are the people who look after their gardens? What colour are the maids? What does that tell us?"

She thought: yes, you're right. And then she thought: David would never say that. Never. That was the difference.

"We had a Jamaican lady working for us," he said. "She was with us until a year or so ago. She was substitute grandmother. The kids still miss her."

"They would."

There was a brief moment of silence. He took a sip of his drink. "That poor woman ..."

"Bella?"

"Mrs Rosales."

"Yes, Bella."

He looked up at the ceiling. "It makes my blood boil."

She waited for him to continue.

"I assume that her employers know what's what. I assume that somebody told them what she needed."

"I believe they did. I only heard about it from Margaret – the woman who helps me. She implied that they just couldn't be bothered."

He shook his head in disbelief. "It could be too late, you know. She may have to lose the leg anyway."

"Well, at least you'll have tried. This person in Kingston – who is he?"

"He's a general surgeon – an increasingly rare breed. He does anything and everything. He used to be in one of the big hospitals in Miami but he retired early and went off to this clinic in Kingston. They're Lutherans, I believe. Missionaries. People like that still exist."

"Do you think he'll be able to help?"

He nodded. "I phoned him just before I came here. He says that he'll see her tomorrow. We took the liberty of booking her on the Cayman Airways flight first thing. I've got my nurse to go round and let her know."

She told him that she would reimburse him for the flight, and he thanked her. "It's not all that uncommon, you know," he said.

"Infections like that?"

"Yes. But I meant it's not uncommon for people to let their domestic workers fend for themselves. I see those people every day of the week. Filipina maids, any number of Jamaicans, Haitians – the lot."

She said that she had heard about the way he helped. "It's very good of you ..."

He brushed aside the praise. "I have to do it. It's my job. I'm a doctor. I'm not a hero or anything like that. That's not the way it is, you know. You just do what you were trained to do – same as anybody."

She watched him. She could tell that he was uncomfortable talking about his work, and she decided to change the subject. Although they had known one another for years, she knew very little about him. She knew that he was British, that Alice was Australian, and that they kept to themselves much of the time. Apart from that, she knew nothing. She asked him the obvious question – the one that expatriates asked each other incessantly. How did you end up here?

He smiled. "The question of questions. Everybody asks it, don't they? It's as if they can hardly believe that anybody would make a conscious, freely made choice to come to this place."

"Well, it's what we all think about, isn't it?"

He agreed. "I suppose it is. In so far as we have any curiosity about our fellow islanders. I'm not sure if I find myself wanting to know about some of them." He hesitated. "Does that sound snobbish?"

"It depends on which ones you're thinking of."

"The rich ones," he said. "I find their shallowness distasteful. And they worship money."

"Then it doesn't sound at all snobbish. And anyway, we all know why they're here. It's the others who are interesting – the people who've come from somewhere else for other reasons. Not just because they're avoiding tax."

He looked doubtful. "Are there many of those?"

"Some people come for straightforward jobs. David did." She felt that she had to defend her husband, who was not as obsessed with money as many of the others were. He was interested in *figures*, and there was a difference.

He was quick to agree. "Of course. I wasn't talking about people like David."

She decided to be direct. "So how did you end up here?"

He shrugged. "Ignorance."

"Of what?"

"Of what I was coming to. You know, when I saw the advertisement in the *British Medical Journal*, the ad that brought me here, I had to go off and look the Caymans up in the atlas – I had no idea where they were. I thought they were somewhere in the South Pacific, you know. I thought they were somewhere down near Samoa. That shows how much I knew."

"So you took a job?"

"Yes. I had just finished my hospital training in London. I was offered the chance to go on to a surgical job, also in London, but somehow I felt that to do that would be just too obvious. All too predictable. So I looked in the back pages of the BMJ and saw an advertisement from the Caymans government. It was for a one-year job in the hospital – somebody had gone off to have a baby and there was a one-year position. I thought: why not?"

"And so you came out here?"

"Yes. I came to do a job, which I did, and then I met Alice. My job at the hospital came to an end but I applied for a permit to do general practice and I got it. The rest is history, as they say."

She smiled at the expression. *The rest is history*. That meant things that happened – everything that happened. The moss. The acquisitions. Children. Inertia. Love. Despair.

She looked about her. A group of four people – two couples – had come into the bar and had taken their places at a table on the other side of the room. They were locals – wealthy Caymanians who had what David called *that look* about them. They did not carry their wealth lightly. She thought she might have seen one of the women before somewhere, but she could not be sure. People like that kept to themselves, to their own circles; they disliked the expatriates, only tolerating them because they were useful to them; they needed the banks, and trusts, and law firms because without them all they had were mangrove swamps, some beaches, and a reef.

George had said something to her that she had missed while being distracted by the newcomers.

"Sorry," she said. "I wasn't paying attention."

"I said: how long are you and David going to stay?"

She sipped at the drink he had bought her, a gin and tonic in which the ice was melting fast. She shrugged. "Until he retires. Which will be ... heaven knows. Another twenty years? Fifteen?" She put down her glass. "And you?"

"I'd leave tomorrow."

She was surprised, and her surprise showed.

"Are you shocked?" he asked.

"No, not really. It's just that I thought you were so … so settled here. I've always imagined that you and Alice are happy."

For a moment he said nothing. She saw him look out of the window, past the line of white sand on which the hotel lights shone, into the darkness beyond, which was the sea. Then he said, "I only stay because these people – my patients – depend on me. It's an odd thing. I could say to them that I was packing up and leaving, but somehow I can't bring myself to do it. Some of them actually rely on me, you know, and that wouldn't be easy. So if you said to me: here's your freedom, I'd go tomorrow. Anywhere. Anywhere bigger than here. Australia. The States. Canada. Anywhere that's the opposite of a ring of coral and some sand in the middle of the Caribbean."

She stared at him. "You're unhappy?" She had not intended to say it, but the words slipped out.

"Not unhappy in the sense of being miserable. I get along, I suppose. Maybe I should just say that I'd like to be leading another life. But then, plenty of people might say that about their lives."

She looked at his hands. She thought they were shaking. No, perhaps not.

"And Alice?" she said.

He looked back at her. "She's not too unhappy," he said. "She doesn't like this place very much – she's bored with it. But in her case, there's something else that is far more important. You see, Alice is completely in love with me. Completely. Not as most wives are with their husbands – they're friends, they rub along together out of habit and convenience. With her, it's something quite unlike that. She lives for me. I'm her reason. I'm her ... well, I suppose I'm her life."

She whispered now. Nobody could hear them, but the intimacy of the conversation dictated a whisper. "And you? How do you feel?"

He shook his head. "I'm sorry. I wish I could give you a different answer, but I can't. I don't dislike her, but I'm not in love with her. Not like that."

"Like me," she said.

For a moment he did not react, and she wondered whether he had heard. In a way, she hoped that he had not. She should never have said that. It was a denial of her marriage. It was an appalling thing to say. David had done nothing to deserve it – but then Alice had done nothing either. They were both victims.

Then he spoke. "I see," he said. 'That's two of us, then. Trapped."

7

David came home from the office at nine-thirty that night, which was two hours after Amanda had returned from the Grand Old House. She had collected the children from Margaret's care and settled them in their rooms. They were full of pizza and popcorn washed down, she suspected, with coloured and sweetened liquids. But they were tired too: Clover had played basketball with Margaret's niece and Billy had exhausted himself in various energetic games with the dogs. They took no time to drift off, and were both asleep by the time she went down the corridor to check up on them. She liked to stand in the doorway and watch her children as they slept, her gaze lingering on the faces she loved so much. That evening she stood for longer than usual, thinking of the stakes in the game she had started. One ill-thought-out, impulsive act could threaten so much: in flirting with adultery she had thrown her children's futures onto the gaming table, but it was not too late. She would stop it right there, before anything else happened. All she had done was to sit and talk with another man, a doctor to whom she had delivered a patient, who had suggested a drink at the end of a difficult day. That was all. There had been no discreet assignation on the beach; no furtive meeting in a car; they had not so much as touched one another. And nobody had seen them anyway.

She turned out the children's lights and made her way back into the kitchen. She would have to eat alone; David had left a message on the answering machine that they would be getting something sent in to eat at the meeting; there was a restaurant in town that dispatched Thai food in containers to the office when required, at any time of day or night. She would have something simple – scrambled eggs and toast, or spaghetti bolognese: the adult equivalent of nursery food. Then she would have an early night and be asleep by the time he came back.

She ate her simple meal quickly. The night was hot and in spite of the air conditioning her clothes seemed to be sticking to her. She got up from the table, not bothering to clear her plate away – Margaret could do that in the morning. She went outside, out of the chilled cocoon of the house into the hot embrace of the night. It was like stepping into a warming oven: the heat folded about her, penetrated her clothing, made the stone flags under her feet feel like smouldering coals. She stepped onto the lawn; the grass was cool underfoot, but prickly. She walked across it to the pool and looked into the water. A light came on automatically when it grew dark, and so the pool had already been lit for several hours, although there was nobody there to appreciate the cool dappling effect on the water.

She looked into the water, which was clear of leaves, as the pool man had come earlier that day. He took an inordinate pride in his work, spending hours ensuring that every last leaf, every blade of grass or twig that blew into the water was carefully removed. "It must look like the empty sky," he said. "Just blue. Nothing else."

She sat down at the edge of the pool, immersing the calves of her legs in the water. With the day's heat behind it, the water was barely cooler than the surrounding atmosphere, and provided little relief. Swimming now would be like bathing in the air itself.

She sat there for twenty minutes or so, before she arose and crossed to the far side of the garden. Beyond the hedge of purple bougainvillea, she could make out the window of Mr Arthur's study. The lights were blazing out, and she saw Gerry Arthur himself standing with his back to the window. She stood still and watched. He was moving his arms around, as if conducting a piece of music.

She stepped forward. The sound of a choir drifted out into the night. *Carmina Burana* – she recognised it immediately. *O Fortuna!* Mr Arthur raised his hands and brought them down decisively, to bring them up again sharply. She smiled as she watched him, and then turned away.

She went back to the pool and took her clothes off, flinging them carelessly onto one of the poolside chairs. The air was soft on her, and now there was the faintest of breezes, touching her skin as a blown feather might, almost imperceptibly. She stepped into the pool and launched herself into the water. She thought again of the Hockney paintings of the boys in the swimming pool, brown under the blue water. She ducked her head below the surface and propelled herself towards the far side of the pool. She thought of George. She imagined that he was here with her, swimming beside her. She turned in the water, half-expecting to see him. He would be naked, as she was. He would be tanned brown, like Hockney's California boys, and youthful. He would be beautiful.

She surfaced. She had shocked herself. *I am swimming by myself. I'm married. I have children. I have a husband.*

When David returned she was still in the pool. He saw her from the kitchen and he called out to her from the window before he came out to join her. He had a beer with him that he drank straight from the bottle. He raised it to her in greeting.

"They settled their differences," he said. "I thought it was going to be acrimonious, but it wasn't. The lawyers were disappointed, of course. They were hoping that the whole thing would end up in litigation." He paused. He had suddenly noticed she was naked. "Skinny dipping?"

She moved to the end of the pool, where she could sit, half lie, on one of the lower concrete steps.

"It was so hot."

He fingered at the collar of his shirt. "Yes. Steaming."

He took a swig of his beer.

She said, "The kids ate at Margaret's tonight. She filled them up with pizza. Do you know how many calories there are in an eighteen-inch pizza?"

"A couple of thousand. Too many, anyway. And heaps of sodium. And what do you call those fats? Saturated?"

"I wish she'd give them something healthy," she said. "Vegetables. Soup. That sort of thing."

"Oh well," he began, and then continued, "Why did they eat there?"

"Because I was late back. I took Mrs Rosales to have her leg looked at. I told you, didn't I? Margaret spoke to me." She had mentioned something to him, but could not recall exactly what she had said.

He took another swig of beer. "Took her to the hospital?"

"No." She tried to sound casual. "I took her to see George Collins. He takes people like that. He takes anybody who hasn't got insurance."

"When?" he asked.

"When what?"

"When did you take her?"

"Late afternoon."

He moved his chair forward and slipped out of his shoes and

socks. He put his feet into the water, not far from her. "And then?" he asked.

She moved her hands through the water, like little underwater ailerons, playing. The movement made ripples, which in turn cast shadows on the bottom of the pool, little lines, like the contour lines on a chart. She was not sure whether his question was a casual one; whether he was merely expressing polite interest, or whether he really wanted to know. So she said nothing, concentrating on the movement of her hands, feeling the water flow through the separated fingers like a torrent through a sluice. Water could be used in massage; the French went in for that, she thought: they had themselves sprayed with powerful jets of seawater. It was meant to do something for you; provoked sluggish blood into movement, perhaps. Thalassotherapy.

He repeated the question. "And then?"

She looked up at him, and saw that he was not really looking at her, but was staring up at the moving leaves of the large sea-grape tree. The breeze, hardly noticeable below, seemed stronger among the highest branches of the tree.

"And then what?" She needed time to think.

He looked down and met her eyes. His expression was impassive. "And then what did you do? After you'd taken what's-her-name …"

"Mrs Rosales," she said quickly, seeing her opportunity. "Bella Rosales. I think she prefers Bella. She's Honduran – the usual story – children over there being looked after by grandmother. Her leg …"

"Yes," he said. "But your day – what happened afterwards?"

"I came home," she said. It was not a lie, she told herself, as she had come home – eventually.

"But you didn't go to fetch the kids?"

She frowned. Why would he ask that?

"I did. Later. I let them eat at Margaret's."

"I see." He paused. His beer was almost finished now, and he tilted the bottle back to drain the last few drops. "You didn't go anywhere else?"

She felt her heart beating wildly within her. She had been seen. Somebody had said something.

"No." This time the lie was unequivocal.

He turned round. "I'm going in. I'm tired."

There was nothing in his tone of voice to give away what he was thinking.

"David ..."

"Yes?"

She looked at him. She would tell him. She would say that she had forgotten. She had been invited by George to have a drink because he had had a wretched day and needed to talk to somebody. But she could not. It was too late. He would never believe her if she said she had forgotten the events of a few hours before. And he did not look suspicious or offended; he did not look like a man who had just established that his wife was lying to him.

"Why don't you join me in here? The water's just right. And Tommy did the pool today. It's perfect."

He hesitated.

"Why not?" He always slept better if he had a swim just before going to bed. It was something to do with inner core temperature; if it was lowered, sleep came more easily.

He took off his clothes; she was aware of his familiar body. He joined her. He put his arm about her shoulder, wet flesh against wet flesh.

8

"Why the tennis courts?"

Teddy had wanted to know. It would take twenty minutes to ride there on their bicycles, and the Saturday morning was already heating up.

"You can die of thirst," he said. "You know that? You can die of thirst if you ride for a long time in the heat. My cousin had a friend who died of de-something ..."

"Dehydration," said Clover. "And don't be stupid. Nobody dies of dehydration these days. It's like being eaten by a lion. It's one of things that used to happen, but don't happen any more."

Teddy looked indignant. "He did. He did die from dehydration. You can see it on his gravestone at West Bay. I promise you."

Clover smiled. "So it says *died of dehydration*, does it? Gravestones never say things like that. They just say *dead*. That's all they say. Then they give the date you were born and the date you died, and maybe something about Jesus and God. That's all."

Teddy looked sullen. "I'm not a liar."

She was conciliatory, and had intercepted a warning look from James. "Maybe he died a bit from dehydration. Maybe there were other things. You can die from two things, you know. Sometimes as many as three things."

"You get bitten by a snake and then a lion eats you on the way to hospital," suggested James. "That's two. You might also get rabies from the lion."

They thought about this. "Anyway," said Clover decisively. "I'll take a water bottle with me and if you get thirsty on the way you can have a drink. We have to go there, you see."

"Why?"

She explained carefully, enunciating each word for Teddy's complete understanding. "Because that's where they all are on Saturday morning. They have this tennis league, you see. All of them."

"Not my mum and dad."

"No," she said. "Not yours. But for the moment we're only watching my mum, remember. She's there, and all her friends. We can watch them. There's a really good place for us to hide – it's a big hedge and nobody would see us in there. Or we can climb one of those big trees and look down on the tennis club. They wouldn't see us there either."

"There might be iguanas," said Teddy. The island was populated by fecund iguanas that feasted on the leaves of trees.

"That's another thing that could kill you," offered James. "If an iguana bites you in the right place, you can die. Not everybody knows it, but it's true."

"Nonsense," said Clover. "You're frightening Teddy."

Amanda sat on the veranda of the tennis club. It was cool there under the broad-bladed ceiling fans; there was shade and there were languid currents of air, while outside under the sun the members of a foursome exerted themselves. There were shouts of exasperation, of self-excoriation; somebody's game was not up to scratch. *I'm sorry, partner. I don't know what's happened to my game. Never mind, never mind.*

She had completed her own game of doubles and had played well, pushing their team a step or two up the club league tables. She was pleased; lessons with the club coach were paying off, as David had said they would. Money well spent, he said.

She was holding a glass of lime soda in which a chunk of ice cracked like a tiny iceberg. She was thinking of the day ahead: Billy was with Margaret on an outing to the dolphin park. She disapproved of the capture of dolphins and did not want to go, but he had set his heart on it. Everybody at school had been; everybody else had been allowed to go, and so Margaret had volunteered. Clover was up to something with James; off on her bicycle somewhere. That, at least, was the benefit of living on a small island; they were safe to wander; they had a degree of freedom that city children could only dream of. In New York there had been Central Park, but it had only been visited under the eyes of parents; there had been skating at the Rockefeller Center; there had been blissful summer weeks at a camp in Vermont. But there had been no individual expeditions to the corner store; no aimless wandering down the street; no outings without watchful adults. At least not until the teenage years, when things changed, even if the world suddenly became less exciting than it had been before.

She would go back to the house and shower before going to the supermarket to stock up with provisions for the weekend. After that ... She kept a diary near the telephone and she envisaged the page for today. There was something at six-thirty – one of those invitations that pointedly did not include dinner. She remembered the name of the hosts: the Hills. They were white Jamaicans who had got out when most of their fellow white Jamaicans had left, cold-shouldered out of the only country they knew, fleeing from the growing violence and lawlessness. There had been a diaspora – some had gone to the United States and Britain; others took the shorter step to the Caymans, where the climate was the same and political conditions kinder. They also fitted in better there: the Caymanians understood them and they understood the Caymanians. The other expatriates – the Australians, the Americans, the British – were not sure how to take them. Here were people who seemed to have a lot in common with them but spoke with a West Indian lilt in their voice, who had been in the Caribbean for six or more generations. They were different.

There would be the Hills' drinks party and then a cooling swim at home, followed by a movie that David would go to sleep in front of; and then the day would end. Another Saturday, like all the other Saturdays.

She watched the players on the court. It was getting too hot to play, really, even in December, and they were all slowing down, hardly bothering to run for the ball. Easy returns were missed because it was just too much effort to exert oneself sufficiently. The score wandered aimlessly.

"Far too hot for tennis, isn't it?"

She looked round. George was standing behind her. He was dressed in a pair of khaki chinos and a blue T-shirt. She realised that she had never seen him in casual attire and had pictured him only in his more formal working clothes.

She laughed. "I played earlier. I'm glad I did."

He drew up a chair and sat down. As he did so, she glanced along the veranda to see who else was there. There was a woman she knew she would see at the Hills' later that day – she was very close to their hosts, a fellow Jamaican exile. There was that teacher from the prep school, the man who taught art, she thought, or was it gymnastics? She did not know the others, although she had seen them at the club before. Nobody seemed to be paying any attention to her, or to George.

"I didn't know you played," she said. She had never seen him at the tennis club before.

He was holding his car keys and he fiddled with these as he replied. "I don't. I was driving past. I noticed your car."

She caught her breath. It was not accidental; he had sought her out.

He waited for a moment before continuing. "So I thought I'd drop by. I was going somewhere else."

"Yes?"

"I sold the yacht and bought an old powerboat. It's seen better days, but it goes. I don't know if you'd heard."

She shook her head. "No."

"I thought maybe James had mentioned something to Clover. He's terribly proud of it." He slipped the keys into his pocket. "They seem to spend a lot of time together, those two."

"They're very friendly. There's a bit of hero-worship going on, I think."

He smiled broadly. "Oh? Him or her?"

"Girl worships boy, I think."

"Childhood friendships," he said. "They might not find it so easy when they hit adolescence. Friendship becomes more complicated then."

"Your boat ..."

"Is nothing special. I can't afford anything expensive. And it's not a sailing boat like the one David and I went out in. It's a knockabout old cruiser with an outboard that's seen better days. It can get out to the reef and back, but that's about it."

She said that she thought that this was all one needed. "Where else is there to go?" she asked.

"Precisely."

"Those great big monsters ..."

"Gin palaces."

"Yes. Why do people need them?"

He smiled. "They can go to Cuba. Or to Jamaica. But it's really all about extensions to oneself, to one's ego. Those are *look at me* boats." He paused. "I was just heading over there. To the boat. Why not come and see it? We could go over to Rum Point. Or out to the reef if you liked."

She had not been prepared for an invitation and it took her some time to answer. She should say no; she should claim, quite rightly, that she had to go to the supermarket. But now, in his presence, she found it impossible to do what she knew she should do.

"How long would it take?"

"As long or as short a time as you want. Fifteen minutes to get there. Ten minutes to get things going. Then forty minutes out and forty minutes in, depending on the wind and what the sea's doing."

She looked at her watch.

"What's everybody doing?" he asked. She realised that this was his way of asking where David was.

"I think that Clover's with James. Out on their bicycles, I think. Billy's at that dolphin place with Margaret. David's working."

"Does he ever take any time off?"

"Sundays, usually. Otherwise … no, he's pretty busy." She looked at him. His eyes were registering pleasure at what she said.

"How about it?"

The sea was calm as they edged out into the sound. They had boarded the boat in the canal along which he moored it – a thin strip of water that provided access to four or five rather run-down houses. Dogs barked from the bank as the boat made its way towards the sea; a large Dobermann, ears clipped, kept pace with them, defending its territory with furious snarls.

She pointed to one of the houses. "Who lives in these places?" she asked.

"You can tell from the dogs," he said. "That Dobermann belongs to a man who owns two liquor stores, and a bar." He made a calming gesture towards the dog. "Dogs are aspirational here. Like boats."

She laughed. "That's his boat there?" She pointed to a gleaming white vessel. A towering superstructure was topped with a bristling forest of aerials and fishing rods.

"Must be."

Once in the sound he opened the throttle and the boat surged forward across the flat expanse of sea. The sky was high and empty of all but a few cumulus clouds on the horizon, off towards Cuba. The water was a light turquoise colour, the white sand showing a bare six feet below. Here and there, patches of undulating dark disclosed the presence of weed. In the distance, a line of white marked their destination, the reef that protected the sound from the open sea beyond. That was the point at which the seabed began to drop until, a few hundred yards further out, it reached the edge of the deep and fell away into hundreds of feet of darkness. The dive boats went there, dropping their divers down the side of a submarine cliff. It was dangerous: every so often divers went down and did not come up; nitrogen-drunk on beauty, they went too deep and forgot where they were.

It was hard to make oneself heard against the roar of the engine. He signalled to her where they were going, and she strained to make out the break in the reef that provided a passage out into the open sea. A small cluster of boats congregated not far away – the boats that took people out to see the school of giant sting-rays that swam into the sound to be fed by the boatmen. The rays, accustomed to people, would glide obligingly round the legs of swimmers, taking fish from the hands of the guides. They had taken the children there on numerous occasions – it was one of the few outings the island afforded – and the memory reminded her that she was a mother. She looked away, and thought: *I should ask him to go back.* She wondered why she had said yes to this. It was … what was the right word for it? Folly. That was it. Folly.

He had slowed the boat to negotiate the difficult passage between the outcrops of coral that made up the reef. It was a clear enough route, and everybody who took a boat out there learned it soon and easily enough. One had to line up several points and keep a careful eye on which way the current was flowing. One had to read the sea, which provided all the necessary signs, particularly on a calm day like this.

"Are you all right with this?" she asked as he steered them towards the gap.

"Yes," he said. "I've done it a few times. You have to watch out, but it's simple enough."

"I won't distract you."

She looked over the side of the boat. The water was shallow enough to stand in, she thought. There was weed, lines of drifting black. A large shell, she thought – a conch, perhaps; a blur of white against the sand. There was a flash of colour as a school of bright blue fish darted past. There was the shadow of the boat on the seabed below.

"There." He had brought them through, and the reef and the breaking waves were suddenly behind them. He opened the throttle again to put water between them and the coral. The sea now was a different colour – a darker blue – and it was rougher too, with a swell bowling in towards them.

He throttled back, making the bow drop down. Then, glancing at a dial on the console, he switched the engine off entirely.

"We might as well conserve fuel. These big outboards are thirsty."

She leaned back against her seat and closed her eyes. She felt the sun on her face; the breeze too. There was silence.

"It's the peace, isn't it?" she muttered, to herself as much as to him. "It's the peacefulness."

She opened her eyes. He was struggling with the catch of a small cool-box that he had brought with them.

"Somebody gave me a bottle of champagne," he said. "A grateful patient."

The catch shifted and the champagne was revealed. Two glasses nestled against the ice, alongside the bottle. She wondered why he had packed two glasses. He had had the cool-box with him when he had met her at the tennis club, but he would not have known that she was there. So this could not have been planned for her. For his wife? For Alice?

The cork popped, shooting up into the air to fall into the sea beside them. She watched it floating away on a swell.

"I didn't mean that to happen," he said. "I disapprove of people who shake champagne and pop the corks. It's one of the biggest causes of eye injury there is." He grinned. "Not that I'm a spoil-sport."

He handed her a glass of champagne. "Here. For you."

She took the glass, which was cold to the touch. She raised it to her lips. It's too late, she thought. This is it.

He took a sip. "You don't mind, do you?" he asked.

"Mind what? Being here? Drinking champagne instead of being at the supermarket?"

He looked serious. "You don't mind that I asked you?"

She shrugged. "Why should I?"

He was studying her reaction. "Because I can't pretend that I didn't hope that I would find you at the tennis club."

For a while she said nothing. It thrilled her: she meant something to him. There was no dismay; just pleasure.

When she spoke the words, it seemed to her, came from somewhere else.

"I hadn't envisaged this happening. But it happens, doesn't it? It … well, it comes over one. I never thought it would. I never thought about it. It just happens."

He nodded. "I hadn't anticipated this either."

"So what do we do?"

The question hung in the air.

"Do?" he said. "I hadn't thought that far."

"Neither had I." She put down her glass. "Because we both have children to think about."

"Yes," he said. "And others."

"By that, you mean …"

She thought that he did not want her to see his wince, but she did. "Alice and David."

It was a mistake, she thought, to mention the names. They had not been present until then, but now they were. And there were only two glasses of champagne.

She drew in her breath. "I think maybe we shouldn't take this any further. I'm sorry."

His mouth opened slightly. She saw that he was gripping the glass tightly, as his knuckles were white. *I've said the wrong thing. It's entirely the wrong thing.*

"Is that what you feel?"

She nodded, and glanced at her watch. "I think it would have been nice. But it can't be. It just can't."

"If that's what you feel ..."

"It is. I'm really sorry, George. I wish that I were free to say yes. I wish that. But I'm not. And I don't think you're free either."

He looked down at the deck. "You're probably right." He drained his glass and put it back into the cool box. Then, picking up the bottle of champagne, he looked at it, held it up against the sun, and then poured it out over the side of the boat. She watched in astonishment, noticing the tiny bubbles, visible against the surface of the sea for a few instants before they disappeared.

"I'm so sorry," she said.

He replaced the bottle and took her glass from her.

"You don't have to say sorry," he said. "I'm the one who should apologise."

"No. You don't have to."

He reached for the ignition. "I suggest we write the whole thing off to experience. That's the civilised way of dealing with these things, I think."

It could have been said bitterly, but she did not detect any bitterness in his voice. He was a kind man, she thought. He was exactly what she thought, and hoped, he was.

9

When George turned the key in the ignition, the outboard engine spluttered into life briefly, but did not catch. He attempted to start it again. Sometimes it took a second try for the fuel to get through; a small blockage, a bubble of air could starve the injectors of fuel but these would right themselves. This time there was no response at all. He looked down at the safety-cord – this was a small key-like device that operated against a sprung switch and had to be in place for the engine to fire. It was correctly slotted in. He tried once more, and again there was no response.

She had not noticed the first failure, but now she did.

"Trouble?"

He raised an eyebrow. "I don't know. It won't start."

"Are we out of fuel?"

He pointed to the gauge. "We've got at least ten gallons. Maybe more."

"Perhaps you should try again."

He reached forward and turned the key. There was complete silence.

"I can check the batteries. A lead might have detached itself."

He opened a hatch, exposing two large twelve-volt batteries. All four leads were in position, and secure. He tried the key again, with the same result.

She glanced over her shoulder. After they had cleared the passage, they had gone half a mile or so out onto the open sea. Now, carried by the swell, they were little more than several hundred yards off the line of surf marking the location of the reef. In ten minutes or so, possibly less, they would have reached the point where the waves would carry them onto the reef itself.

"Have you got a radio?"

He shook his head. "I've got my phone. We're not too far out. We'll get reception."

She felt a surge of relief. "Then phone somebody."

"Who?"

She frowned. "The police. They'll know what to do."

He reached into his pocket to retrieve his phone. As he did so, he looked about, scanning the sea. On the other side of the reef, in the protected waters of the sound, he could see three or four boats still bobbing at anchor round the sting-ray feeding grounds. He could make out the heads of swimmers in the water.

"Could we attract their attention?" she asked.

"I'm not carrying any flares. If we had a flare they'd see it. But I haven't."

She stood up and looked over in the direction of the knot of boats. She had been frightened, but the human presence not too far away reassured her. If the worst came to the worst, they could abandon ship and swim back through the passage in the reef. They would be seen then, or they could even swim over to join the boats at anchor. It was not as if they were far out at sea; and the water, as usual, was invitingly warm.

She saw that George was looking anxiously at the reef, to which they were slowly being carried by the swell. She looked down: they were in about forty feet of water, she thought, but as they approached the reef that would diminish. Could they not anchor and then wait for help – boats regularly used the entrance to the sound and they would not have to wait too long.

"Your anchor," she suggested. "Couldn't we …"

"Yes," he said. "I was thinking that."

He moved to the bow and opened a locker. Reaching in, he

lifted out a rather shabby-looking anchor to which a line of rusty chain was attached. He looked over the side of the boat.

"We'll have to get a bit closer to the reef," he said. "It's too deep here."

The swell seemed to pick up, and they found themselves being pressed closer and closer to the breaking waves and the jagged points of coral. When they were only a few boat's lengths from the first of the outcrops, George heaved the anchor over the side, paying out the chain and line.

She felt the boat shudder as the anchor line took the strain.

"She might drag a bit," he said. "We'll have to watch."

But it held, and the boat was soon pointed into the incoming swell, riding it confidently.

George sat down. He wiped his brow and smiled at her. "There we are. Emergency over."

She scanned the sea. "No sign of anything."

He seemed confident that help would not be long delayed. "Something will come by. A fishing boat. A yacht. Less than an hour, I'd say." He looked at her apologetically. "I'm sorry about all this. You went off to play tennis and ended up shipwrecked."

"Not quite."

"Near enough. And I rather wish I hadn't disposed of the rest of the champagne."

She made a sign to indicate she did not mind. "I'm fine."

He was about to say something, but did not. She was pleased that he did not, as she did not wish to discuss what had gone before. Some lovers, she thought; some affair.

She steered the conversation to neutral topics. They discussed the plan to extend the system of canals to sensitive mangrove swamps. They discussed the ambitions of the developers who were setting out to cover the island with concrete and pastel-coloured condos. He became animated on the subject of corruption. She listened, and found herself agreeing with everything he said. David was far less harsh in his judgement of developers; in fact, he spoke up in favour of them. That was the difference.

She looked at her watch. They had been anchored for forty-five minutes and there had been no sign of any boat. It was barely noon, and there were another six hours of daylight, but what if nobody came? Who would report them missing? David had no idea where she was and she did not want to ask George whether Alice knew that he was going out in the boat. If she did, then she would raise the alarm and they would send out a search party, but if she did not know, then it could be the next day before anybody came and found them. Did they have enough water, she wondered. And there was no food, although one could last for a long time without anything to eat.

"You aren't worried?" he asked.

"Not really." She hesitated. "No, maybe a bit."

"We'll be all right. In fact …" He broke off, as he had seen something and was standing up, shading his eyes with his hand. "Yes. Help's on its way."

She stood up too, and he pointed out the direction in which she should look. He took her hand in his, to do so, which was not strictly necessary – he could have pointed. But she felt a stab of excitement at his touch.

There was a boat in the distance – a powerboat churning the sea behind it, heading their way.

She squeezed his hand in relief, and he returned the pressure. Then he leaned over and kissed her gently on the cheek.

"See," he said. "We're saved."

She felt herself blushing at the kiss, like an innocent schoolgirl. He should not have done it, she thought, because they had agreed, had they not, that they were not going to take this further. But she was glad that he had because the kiss had felt so wrong and so right at the same time.

As the boat approached, George began to move his arms from side to side in the maritime gesture of distress. Figures could now be made out on the deck of the other boat and there was a response. The boat slowed and changed course towards them.

"Thank God," said George.

"A relief," said Amanda.

"I'm going to have to get a new outboard after this," George said.

The other boat was a rather larger cruiser, set up for deep-sea fishing, although not sporting any rods. Gingerly it came alongside, taking care to leave sufficient distance so as not to be pushed by the swell on to the anchored boat.

"What's the trouble?" asked the man at the controls.

"Engine failure," shouted George. "We'll need a tow."

The man nodded. "We'll throw you a line. Ready?"

Amanda had been looking at the other skipper. Now she looked at the crew, of whom there were four. With a start she recognised John Galbraith, one of David's partners in the firm. He saw her at much the same time as she saw him, and he waved.

"Amanda!" he called out.

She acknowledged the call.

"I didn't expect to see you," he shouted out. "Are you all right?"

She cupped her hands and shouted a reply. "Fine. Absolutely fine."

John gave the thumbs-up sign and then busied himself fixing

the line to a cleat at the stern of the boat. Then the other end of the line was thrown across to George. It went into the sea the first time, but was retrieved and thrown again. This time it was caught and secured to the bow of the stricken vessel. The anchor was pulled up and the rescuing boat took the strain.

Progress under tow was slow, but once through the passage in the reef there was little to do but to sit back and wait. Amanda went to the stern and sat by herself, deep in thought. The implications of what had happened were slowly sinking in. The odds against being rescued by somebody she knew were not all that high. The island was small and people knew one another. If she had imagined that she could go anywhere – anywhere at all – and not be spotted, then she was mistaken. Yet it was particularly bad luck that it should be John, of all people. He and David saw one another every day, for most of the day; he would be bound to mention that he had rescued his colleague's wife.

She felt raw inside. Dread, she thought. That's what dread feels like. Rawness. Hollowness. She would have to speak to John. She would have to ask him not to say anything. And that meant that she would have to confess that her presence on George's boat was being kept secret from David. It was nothing short of an admission of adultery.

The rescuing boat took them all the way back to the canal. One of their crew jumped out onto the dock to pull them in, and they were soon safely attached. Amanda went ashore. The other boat was standing off and was about to leave to go back to its own berth at a marina some distance away.

John waved to her. "Happy ending," he called out. "But I'll have to claim salvage from David!"

She shook her head. "No," she called out. "Don't."

He laughed. "Only joking."

The other boat was beginning to pull away. She looked at John desperately. She was unable to shout out a request that he say nothing. She waved again, trying to make a cancelling gesture. He waved back, giving her a thumbs-up sign. Then they moved off, leaving behind them a wake that washed sedately at the edges of the canal. She heard the barking of the liquor store man's Dobermann, and laughter from the other boat.

George was at her side.

"You knew him?"

She nodded miserably. "David's partner."

He was silent for a while. Then: "Oh. Not good."

"No."

He looked at her expectantly. "What do you want me to do?"

"You? Nothing."

She thought of what she should do. She would go back to the tennis club, collect her car, and then drive straight to the Galbraith house and wait for John to come home. She would explain to him that she did not want him to mention to David that she had been out in George's boat. She would tell him the truth; she would explain that there was nothing between them but that she understood that it looked suspicious. She would appeal to him through truthfulness.

10

John Galbraith lived on his own in a house overlooking South Sound. The house was older than others around it, having been built when the land in that area was first cleared. It was modest in scale compared with more recent constructions, and less ostentatious. A recent storm had brought down several of his trees but the house itself was still largely obscured by vegetation when viewed from the road, and it was only once on the driveway that one could see the full charm of the Caribbean-style bungalow. A deep veranda ran the length of the front, giving an impression of cool and shade. The exterior was painted light blue and the woodwork white – a local combination that could still be seen on the few remaining old Cayman cottages. It was a perfect colour scheme for a landscape dominated by sea and sky.

John, who was in his early forties, had been in the Caymans for almost fifteen years, having arrived several years before David and Amanda. He was now the senior local partner in the accountancy firm in which David worked, and would become, so everybody said, an international partner before too long.

He was unmarried – a fact that led to the usual speculation, but none of it substantiated. There were rumours about his private life, of course, about boyfriends, but if these ever reached him, he showed only indifference to gossip, and cheerfully enjoyed the company of women, who found him sympathetic and a good listener.

Amanda encountered John socially at drinks and dinner parties. She and David had been to his house on several occasions, and had entertained him themselves. As a spare man who was good company at a dinner party, he was much in demand by hostesses seeking to balance a table. He could be counted on to talk to any woman he was seated next to without giving rise to any complications. He could be counted upon, too, never to mention business, which formed the core of many of the other men's conversation. People said there had been a tragedy in his life somewhere, but nobody had discovered what it was. There was one wild theory – risible, Amanda thought – that he had killed somebody in New Zealand, where he originally came from, and had come to the Caymans to escape prosecution.

He was not in when Amanda arrived. She had thought that she would probably arrive too early – it would have taken time for them to dock the other boat – but she wanted to be sure that she did not miss him. She had no idea what plans he might have, but she thought there was a danger that he had been invited to the Hills' – she knew he was friendly with them – and she would have to see him before that. At the Hills' it would be too late, as he might say something to David.

She parked her car on his driveway under the shade of a large Flamboyant tree and began her wait. The minutes dragged past; after half an hour, she got out of the car and stretched her legs; after an hour she began to wonder whether she should write him a note and slip it under his front door. It could be brief – a request that he say nothing about seeing her in the boat and offering to give him her reasons later on, when they could meet to discuss it.

She had a notebook with her in the glove compartment of the car, and she took this out and began to compose the note. She was writing this when she heard the car and, looking up, saw John's dark blue Mercedes coming up the drive. He slowed down as he drew level with her and peered into the car. Recognising her, he gave a wave and continued to the garage at the side of the house.

Amanda left her car and walked up the drive to meet him.

"Twice in one day," joked John. "Is everything all right?"

"I wanted to thank you," she said. "But you dashed off."

He smiled, and gestured to the front door. "Come in. I'll make some coffee, or something cooler?"

She followed him into the house.

"I must say," he began, "that I've often thought about what would happen if one lost power out there. I don't have a boat myself, but I'd always have an auxiliary engine if I did. Something to get one back through the reef."

She agreed. "It seems reasonable."

He led her into a sitting room at the front of the house. From the windows at the end of the room, there was a view of a short stretch of grass and then, framed by trees, the sea. On the walls there were paintings on Caribbean themes: a Jamaican street scene, a small island rising sharply out of the sea, a couple of colourful abstracts.

He invited her to sit down while he went to prepare coffee. "Where's David?" he asked. His tone was level. "Working, I suppose."

"Yes."

"Not my fault," he said. "I keep telling him to work less. He puts the rest of us to shame."

"Yes, I think so too. But …"

He looked at her expectantly.

"This isn't easy for me," she said.

He stared at her, and then sat down. He would make the coffee later.

"It's about today? About that business out at the reef?"

She nodded. "I know what you're probably thinking."

He held her gaze. "I try to keep out of other people's private affairs," he said. "It crossed my mind that it was a bit … how should I put it? Surprising that you were out there with … what's that doctor's name again?"

"George Collins."

"Yes. George Collins." He paused. "I hardly know him. I've met him once or twice at the usual functions, but they seem to keep to themselves for the most part, don't they?"

"They do."

He sighed. "I didn't think it was any of my business what was happening on that boat."

"But there wasn't anything happening," she blurted out. "We just went out in the boat together."

He stared at her for a moment, as if he was deciding whether to say something. Then he shrugged. "Well, that's fine then. You've made the point that it was just a casual trip. I'll go and make coffee."

"No," she said. "That's not the point. The point is that David doesn't know that I went out. I didn't tell him."

He stared at her. "Oh."

"Yes. I didn't tell him. George bumped into me at the tennis club and asked me on the spur of the moment." That was not strictly true, she thought, but it would become too complicated if she had to explain further.

"He just suggested it? Like that?"

"Yes." She wondered if that sounded implausible.

He seemed to be weighing up the likelihood of her telling the truth. "So what you're saying is that this was an unplanned outing that you didn't tell David about. And now you think that David will be …"

"Will be suspicious."

He looked out of the window. "You must forgive me," he said. "As a bachelor, I'm not sure that I understand how these things work. Are you saying that a husband would automatically be suspicious if his wife went off on an outing with another man?"

She wanted to laugh. Was he that unaware of how the world worked? "Yes, that's exactly what I'm telling you. And he would be. As would a wife."

"Always?"

She thought about this. "Well, it depends on the circumstances. You couldn't go out for dinner with another man, for example, unless you discussed it with your husband first."

He asked about the position of an old friend of both husband and wife. Could he take the wife out for dinner if the husband was away?

"Of course. An old friend could do that, yes. As I said, it depends on the circumstances."

"Well, that seems reasonable enough. But …" He frowned. "But you're telling me that David would think that you and this doctor … George Collins were having an affair?"

She did not answer him immediately. It was possible that David would not form that impression, but there was a good chance he would. She explained her anxiety to John, who listened attentively. But halfway through her explanation, she faltered.

"I suppose I should tell you the truth."

She saw the effect that this had on him. He drew back slightly, as if offended.

"I would hope you'd tell me the truth," he said stiffly. "Who likes to be lied to?"

"I'm sorry. Of course you wouldn't want to be lied to. The problem is, you see, that I've felt attracted to George Collins. I like him. I'd go so far as to say that I'm interested in him, but I haven't been having an affair with him. We discussed it – yes, we did talk about it, but it hasn't gone anywhere."

He looked at her intently. "I'm sorry that you feel you can't trust me with the truth."

She was aghast. "But what I've just told you is absolutely true."

"Is it?"

She became animated. "Yes, it is. It is the truth."

He held her gaze. There was an odd expression on his face, she thought; it was as if he were just about to pull the rabbit out of the hat.

"Well," he said evenly. "If that were the case, then I must have imagined what I saw from our boat."

She looked puzzled.

"I saw," he continued, "the two people in that boat kissing. I'm sorry, but that's what I saw. I just happened to be looking through my binoculars at the time. We'd seen the signalling and I was interested to see what was going on. I looked through my binoculars."

She stared at him in silence. George had kissed her – that brief, entirely chaste kiss of relief. It was not even on the lips. A kiss on the cheek. And he had been seen.

"That's not what you think it was," she stuttered.

He spread his palms in a gesture of disengagement. "I saw what I saw. Forgive me for jumping to conclusions."

"He kissed me when he saw that you were coming to our rescue. It was the equivalent of … of a hug. That's all. There was nothing more to it than that." She paused. "I promise you, John. I give you my word."

She could tell that he did not believe her. And had she been in his position, she would not have believed herself either.

"Well, I don't think it has anything to do with me," he said. "As I said, I like to avoid getting involved in other people's entanglements. I know that these things happen, by the way. I'm not standing here being disapproving."

"I feel so powerless. I can't make you believe ..."

He interrupted her. "You don't have to make me believe anything, Amanda."

"I'm not cheating on David," she said, putting as much resolution into her voice as she could muster. "I want you to know that."

"Fine. So you've told me."

"But I need to know: will you tell David about what happened today?"

He rose to his feet. His tone now was distant. "I'm sorry, but I'm not going to lie. I know you may have little time for it, but I happen to hold a religious position on these things. I will not tell a lie." He looked at her. "Does that make me sound pompous? Okay, it does. But that's where I stand."

She struggled to control herself. Tears were not far off, she felt, but she did not want to break down. "You don't sound pompous, John. And I'd never ask you to lie. All I'd like to ask you is not to tell him about my being out there in the boat. That's not a lie. It's just ..."

"Concealment?"

She tried to fight back. "We don't have a duty to tell everybody everything. That's not concealment, for heaven's sake."

He seemed to reflect on this. He walked to the window and looked out across the grass to the sea beyond. She thought: he's never been involved in the messiness that goes with relationships. He doesn't know. He's a monk, with a monk's understanding of life, which is not how life is for most of us.

"I'll not say anything," he said after a while. "I won't mention the incident to David, but, and I'm sorry to say you won't make me change my mind on this, if he were to ask me about it, then I would have to tell him the truth." He turned to face her. "And that truth would be the whole truth."

She knew what he meant by this. If he were asked, he would mention the kiss.

She nodded her acceptance. Then she said, "John, may I just say one thing more? I haven't lied to you today. I promise you that. I've got nothing to hide."

He raised an eyebrow. "Apart from what you're hiding from David."

She looked down at the floor. She would not lose her temper.

"You know something?" she said. "You think that you understand things. You don't, you know. You've kept yourself apart from the messy business of being an ordinary human being with ordinary human temptations and imperfections and … and conflicts. You're looking at the world through ice, though, John."

His look was impassive, but she could tell that she had wounded him. She had not meant to do that, and she immediately apologised. "I'm sorry. That came out more harshly than I intended. I'm very sorry."

He held up a hand. "But you're right," he said. "I have kept myself away from these things you mention. But have you any idea – any idea at all – of what that has cost me? You don't know, do you, about how I've come back here sometimes, at night, by myself, and cried my eyes out? Like a boy? You don't know that, do you?"

"I'm sorry, John ..."

He shook his head. "I didn't mean to burden you with that. It's nothing to do with you."

She got up and went towards him. She put an arm around his shoulder, to comfort him. He flinched at her touch.

"I understand," she whispered. "I understand."

"Do you? I don't think people do."

"They do. Some may not, but most do."

After that, they were, for a time, quite silent. She moved away from him and told him that she would not stay for coffee after all. He nodded, and accompanied her, unspeaking, to the door. The heat outside met her like a wall.

11

Teddy's father was arrested four days later. It was done with the maximum, and unnecessary, fuss, with two police cars, sirens wailing, arriving at the front of the house shortly after eight in the morning. Amanda was taking the dog for a walk round the block at the time, and saw what happened.

"They made a big thing of it," she said to David that evening. "There were six or seven of them – one or two senior officers, I think, and the rest constables. It was totally over the top."

He snorted. "Role playing."

"Anyway, they bundled Gerry Arthur out of the house, put him into one of the cars, and then drove off, sirens going full tilt."

"Ridiculous."

"Then one of the constables came out carrying a computer, put that into the other car, and off they went."

"A show – that's what it was."

She looked at her husband. He had a built-in antipathy to officials.

"What was it all about?" she asked. "Have you heard?"

"I met Jim Harris," he said. "He told me that Gerry Arthur is being charged with being party to some fraud or other. Something to do with the scuttling of a ship to get the insurance payment. Apparently that sort of thing happens. You sink your boat and claim the insurance."

"I'm surprised. They go to that Baptist church, don't they?"

David laughed. "Baptists are every bit as capable of sinking ships as anybody else, I suspect. But I wouldn't have thought that Gerry Arthur did that sort of thing anyway. He's one of our clients. We audit his books, and they're always scrupulously clean. This'll be a put-up thing."

She asked him to explain.

"You know what it's like here. You make a remark that offends somebody high up in the political food-chain. All of a sudden, it's discovered that there are problems with your work permit. Gerry has status, I think, which means they can't chuck him out, even if he's not an actual citizen. So the next best thing is to get him into trouble with the police."

She pointed out that it would be difficult to set up the sinking of a ship.

"No," he said. 'The ship would have sunk anyway. So all you have to do is to create some evidence of an instruction to the captain that points to the thing being deliberate. You've got your case. You leak something to the police and they're delighted to get the possibility of a high profile conviction. Off you go."

"What will happen?"

He was not sure. "I heard that they've let him out on bail. They might drop the charges if he agrees to go off to the British Virgin Islands or somewhere like that. It'll die down. It usually does."

"It's very unfair."

"Of course it is."

She looked at him. "To be accused of doing something you haven't done. That must be very hard."

He returned her gaze. "Yes. Certainly." Then he said, "To be accused of doing something you have done – that must be hard as well, don't you think?"

She caught her breath. "Yes, I suppose so."

He was still watching her, and it was at that moment that she became certain that he knew.

Clover said to Teddy: "Your dad was taken off to jail, Teddy. The police came. Is he still in jail?"

The boy bit his lip. "They brought him back. They made a mistake."

"Really? Why did they take him anyway? Was he spying?"

Teddy shook his head. "Don't be stupid."

"It's not stupid. We know there are spies here."

Teddy kicked at the ground in his frustration. "He hadn't done anything. They said he'd sunk one of his boats, but he didn't. You'd have to be stupid to sink one of your own boats."

She nodded. The world of adults was opaque and sometimes difficult to fathom; but the proposition that one would not normally sink one of one's own boats seemed reasonable enough. "I'm sorry for you, Teddy," she said. "It must be awful having your dad taken away by the police."

"Thank you. But he didn't do anything."

Later, she talked to James about it. He agreed with her that the sinking of the boat might just be a cover for the real charge of spying. Now that the police had become involved, though, he thought there was no need to continue with their observations. "It's in their hands now," he pronounced. "We can stop."

He had lost interest, she sensed, and so the notebook, and the photographs they had collected, were filed away in a cupboard in James's room. The photographs, of which there were about fifteen, had been printed on James's computer and labelled with the date, time and place when they had been taken. *At the tennis club, Saturday morning. Suspect 1 gets into the car with Suspect 2.* And *At the tennis club, Suspect 1 talks to Suspect 2. Details of conversation unknown.*

She sensed that he was more concerned with other things. She invited him to the tree-house, but he rarely came now, and when he did, he seemed detached, as if he wanted to be somewhere else. He never stayed long.

She made suggestions. "We could fix the tree-house; I could get some wood. We could take more things up there. If you wanted, I could make you a shelf of your own for your stuff."

He shrugged. "Maybe."

She persisted. "We could take the walkie-talkies up there. I could leave one there and you could take the other to your house. We could speak to each other."

He looked bored. "Out of range," he said. "You have to be able to see the other person, or they don't work. Those are useless walkie-talkies."

He looked at his watch. "I can't stay for long."

She said, "You're always saying that. You're always saying you have to go and do something else."

"I'm not."

"You are. You do it all the time."

He looked at his watch again.

"Well, it's true," he said. "I've got stuff to do."

She felt frustrated at not being able to pin him down. She wanted to have his full attention, but he seemed now to be reluctant to give her that. It was as if he were holding back; as if he were away somewhere, in a different place – a place that she could not get to, or understand. And yet he was not rude to her. He was kind, and, unlike other boys, behaved gently, without any of the pushing or shoving that boys seemed to use. That was part of his appeal – that, and the way he looked. She thought nobody could ever look more beautiful. She had, hidden away, a photograph that she had taken of him without his knowledge.

Amanda sensed her daughter's unhappiness.

"Something's wrong, darling. I can tell."

"Nothing."

"No, you can't just say nothing. If something's wrong, you should tell me about it."

"I told you: everything's fine."

Amanda put an arm about her. "James? Is that it? Has James been nasty to you?"

She shook her head. The denial was genuine. "He's never nasty. He's too nice for that."

"Doesn't want to play any more? Is that it?"

This was greeted with silence, which was an answer in itself. Amanda gave Clover a hug. "My darling, here's something that you're going to have to get used to. Boys are different – they have things that keep them busy and sometimes they don't seem interested in the things that girls want to do. Boys can ignore you when you really want them to take notice. That can be really hard. They break our hearts, you see. Do you know what I'm talking about? They make us girls feel sad because they don't want to be with us. There may be no special reason for that – they might just want to be by themselves. You're just beginning to see this now; when you're a teenager – a bit older, maybe – you're going to see it all much more clearly. And there's no easy answer, no magic wand. I can't make James want to spend time with you. I can't make him be your friend. I wish I could, but I can't."

She nestled into her mother. She just wanted to be James's friend. She just wanted to be with him. He had been happy with that before, but now no longer.

Amanda kissed Clover's forehead. So precious, she thought.

She tried to remember what it had been like at that age. The problem was that we so quickly forgot that even young children have intense feelings for others. Passionate adoration does not suddenly arrive, ready made, when one is fifteen or sixteen – the stage of the first fumbling romance. Falling head over heels for another can occur years earlier, and we would understand these things better if only we bothered to remember. That intensity of feeling for a friend was usually not expressed in any physical way, but it represented a yearning that was already knocking on the door.

12

Clover knew all along that there would come a day when she would have to go away to school. The Cayman Prep School took children up to thirteen before handing them over to the High School. Many children made the transition smoothly and completed their education in the senior division next door, but for a considerable proportion of expatriates the expense of sending children for their secondary education abroad was outweighed by the risks involved in staying. The island had a drug problem, as well as a problem of teenage pregnancy. Stories circulated of girls who had stayed being seen as an easy target by boys from West Bay. Sending children abroad might have its drawbacks, but at least the teenage years would be passed, for the most part, in the supervised conditions of a boarding school. There the day-to-day headaches of looking after adolescents were borne by people paid to bear them – and experienced in doing so.

Clover knew, and accepted that boarding school awaited her. She was ready to go; several girls who had been in the year above her at the Prep School were already there and seemed to enjoy it. They came back each school holidays and were full of stories of a world that seemed to her to be unimaginably exciting and exotic. There were stories of school dances and trips to London. There were accounts of clandestine assignations with boys – meetings that took place under the threat of dire punishment if discovered. It all sounded to her like a rather exciting prison camp in which girls and boys pitted their wits against the guards. But unlike a prison camp, you could have your own pictures on the wall, perfectly good food, and outings, admittedly restricted, to the cinema and shops.

Her parents talked to her about the choice of school. David wanted something in Scotland, and identified a school in Perthshire that seemed to offer everything they wanted. They showed her the pictures in the school brochure.

"You see how attractive it is," said David. "You'd be staying in one of those buildings over there. See? Those are the girls' dormitories."

She looked at the photograph. It was of an alien landscape, all hills and soft colours, but it was a world that she had been brought up to believe was where she belonged. The Caribbean, with its dark greens and light blues, was temporary; this was permanent.

"And that's the pipe band," said Amanda, pointing at one of the photographs. "You can learn the pipes if you like. Or the violin. Or any instrument, really. They have everything."

There were misgivings. "I won't know anybody. Nobody I know is going there."

"You'll make plenty of new friends. It's a very friendly place."

Silence.

"And if I'm sick?"

"Why should you be sick? Anyway, they'll have a sick room. There'll be a nurse. Really, darling, you'll be fine."

"I suppose so."

"What about James?" asked her mother. "He's going off to school too, isn't he?"

James had not told her very much. "I think he's going to a school in England. I don't know what it's called." She looked at her mother. "Couldn't you tell them about Strathearn? Couldn't you show them this?" She pointed to the brochure.

Amanda smiled. "It's nothing to do with us," she said. "They're not Scottish, like Daddy. James's father is English. He'll want James to go somewhere in England. It's only natural."

"But Scotland and England are close together, aren't they? Aren't they next door?"

"They are. But the schools are different, I think. They want him to go to an English school."

"They could change their minds if they saw this brochure."

Amanda looked at her daughter fondly. "You'll be able to see James in the holidays. He'll be here, and so will you. You'll still see him."

Clover became silent. She stared at the photographs of the school and imagined that it was her face in one of the pictures. And standing next to her was not that boy with ginger hair who was in the picture, but James. She wanted to share what lay ahead with him. She did not want to be with strangers.

Her mother touched her arm lightly. "You'll get over it," she whispered.

"Get over what?"

"You'll get over what you feel for James. I know right now he's a very special friend, but we meet other people, you know. There'll be plenty of boys at – different boys. You'll get to know them and they'll be your friends."

She stared at her mother. How could somebody as old as that understand what it was like? What did she know?

That night, lying in her bed, she closed her eyes and imagined, for the first time, that James was with her. It made her feel warm to think of his being at her side, under the covers, as if they were lost children. His feet felt cold as she moved her own feet against his. She held his hand and she listened to his breathing. She told him about her school and he told her about his. They were together and they would stay together until morning. Nobody could take him away from her; no school in England could keep him from her. They would stay together forever. From now on. Forever.

It was the day following the conversation about schools. Amanda and Clover went to the supermarket near the airport to stock up for the week. Outside in the car park, as they were unloading the trolley into the back of the car, a car drew up beside them. A woman got out. Amanda paid her no attention and was surprised when she suddenly realised that it was Alice Collins.

Amanda moved to the side of the car to greet her. "Sorry. I didn't recognise you behind those sunglasses."

Alice took off the sunglasses, folded them, and then placed them in her hip pocket. "Better?"

"Yes. I wasn't paying attention."

She saw that the other woman was not smiling. There was tension in her face.

"Is something wrong?"

Alice turned away; it was as if she had not heard the question. Then, without saying anything, she walked off. Amanda opened her mouth to say something, but Alice had walked round the side of another parked car and was lost to view. From within the car, she could hear Clover operating the electric window.

"What did Mrs Collins say?"

"She didn't say anything," said Amanda. "She's in a rush, I think."

She finished the unpacking of her trolley. She felt quite weak with the shock of the deliberate snub. It was the feeling one has after some driving error on one's part brings a snarl from another driver – a feeling of rawness, of surprise at the hostility of another.

Clover was listening to music, her ear buds in place. Amanda drove off, her heart still racing after the encounter with Alice. She must know; but how? Had John said something? She was not confident that he could be trusted; it was not that he would gossip – there was a far greater possibility that he would speak about what he had seen on principle. But if he spoke to anybody, would it not be to David, rather than to Alice? She considered the possibilities. One was that John was friendly with Alice and felt that he had a duty to warn her. Or he could have spoken to David, who had told Alice in order to get her to warn George off. That was feasible only if David would *want* to warn George off, which was far from clear. Another possibility was that George had decided to make a clean breast of things and had told Alice that he had almost embarked on an affair but had not done so. He might have done that had he thought that news would leak out somehow – probably through John – and that it would be better to raise the matter himself rather than to protest innocence once his wife became aware of it.

"Look out!"

Clover had spotted the car making the dangerous attempt at overtaking. Amanda pulled over sharply, and the two vehicles that had been heading straight for one another avoided collision by a matter of a few inches.

"Didn't you see him?"

Amanda looked in the mirror. The other car, now behind them, was being driven erratically – far too fast, and halfway into the other lane.

"That was his fault. He shouldn't have been overtaking there. The road's clearly marked."

"Maybe he's drunk."

"Could be."

They drove on in silence. As was always the case with such things, notions of what she should have done came after the event. She should have pursued Alice and asked her what was wrong. She should have said to her that whatever she had heard was not the real truth – the real truth was that there was nothing between her and George and there never had been; accepting the brush-off was tantamount to an admission of guilt.

Clover switched off her music. She looked at her mother.

"I hate this place," she said.

Amanda turned to look at her daughter. "What place?"

"Here. This. This whole place. Cayman."

"I thought you liked it."

Clover shook her head vigorously. "There's nothing to do. And I've got no friends."

Amanda's gaze returned to the road ahead. The plane from Cayman Brac, a small twelve-seater, was coming in to land; its shadow passed across the road and the mangrove swamp on the other side.

"You need to get away to school. That's soon enough." She paused. "And you have got friends. You've got Holly …"

"She doesn't like me any more. She spends most of her time with that American girl."

"You've got James."

This was greeted with silence.

Amanda shot her a glance. "You still like James, don't you?"

Clover moved her head slightly.

Amanda spoke gently. "He's special to you, isn't he? It's good to have a special friend."

Suddenly Clover turned to her mother. "Do you think that

when we're both grown up …"

"Yes? When you're both grown up?"

"That maybe James and I will get married? Do you think that might happen?"

Amanda suppressed a smile. "Possibly, but it's far too early to even think about that. You never know whom you're going to marry. But what you really want to do is to marry somebody who's kind. That's the most important thing, you know. They don't have to be good-looking or rich or anything like that – but they have to be kind."

"James is kind."

"Yes, I'm sure he is. But it's very early to talk about what may or may not happen. You're going to meet plenty of other boys, you know, and it's highly likely that some of them will be every bit as nice as James. You've got years and years to meet other people, and so you shouldn't make your mind up too early."

"But he's the one I want."

"But that could change. You might think very differently when you're … say, twenty-five, twenty-six. You may have very different ideas."

"I won't."

"I think you'll find that you will."

"No."

The conversation ended there. They had reached the turn off to their house and Clover would shortly have to get out to open the gate.

Over the next few weeks, James's visits, which had become less frequent anyway, stopped altogether. Clover waited several days before summoning up her courage to call him on his phone.

He sounded friendly enough when he answered, but when she asked if he would like to come round to listen to some music, he sounded wary.

"Maybe I'd better not," he said.

"Why not? Just for half an hour?"

"Because ..."

"Because what?"

He did not reply immediately, but after a while he said, "Ted's coming round."

She waited for him to invite her too, but he did not.

"I could come too."

This was greeted with silence.

She tried again. "I could come, if you'd like."

She heard his breathing. "Actually, Clover, it was just me and Ted. We were going to do some things."

"What things?"

"Ted's got a metal detector."

She persisted. "Couldn't I ..."

"No, Clover, sorry. Maybe some other time."

There was silence.

"Don't you like me any more?" It was a wild gamble. He could easily say no, he did not, and that would be the end of the friendship. But he did not. "Of course I like you, it's just that my mother says that you and I should ... shouldn't spend so much time together."

She absorbed this.

"What's it got to do with her?"

He sounded surprised. "She says ..."

"You don't have to do everything your mother tells you, James." And with that she hung up. She hoped that he would call her back, chastened, apologetic, but he did not. She sank her head in her hands. Why did she feel so empty, so unhappy? Why should a boy do this? She had never asked for this to happen; all she wanted was to be his friend, forever if possible, but at least for that day, for that moment. She wanted to see him again and listen to the way he laughed. She wanted him to look at her and smile. She wanted it to be the same as it always had been. Which is, of course, what we all want. We all want love, friendship, happiness to last forever, to be as it was before.

13

There was nothing in David's behaviour to indicate that he knew. She watched him closely over the days that followed the encounter with Alice in the car park. But there was nothing unusual in the way in which he spoke to her; nothing to suggest a change in the polite, but somewhat distant, relations between them. He was busy preparing for a business trip to New York that would take place two weeks later – a trip that he said would be awkward. There were Internal Revenue Service enquiries into the affairs of one of the firm's clients and he had been requested to attend a hearing. It was entirely voluntary – the Cayman Islands were outside the jurisdiction of the American tax authorities, but the client was asserting his innocence vigorously and had waived any privilege of confidentiality. David was sure that the client had nothing to hide, but he knew that he would be treated as a hostile witness, that he would be disbelieved.

She heard that John Galbraith would be going too. He disclosed this casually, but her heart thumped when she heard it.

"Why does he have to go? It's your client, isn't it?"

"I took him over from John," he replied. "He looked after him for part of the period they're interested in."

She searched around for something to say. "John would be good in court …"

"It's not actual court proceedings. It's an enquiry."

"He'd be good at that."

He was looking at her. They were sitting in the kitchen; he had just returned from work – late – and was drinking a beer at the kitchen table. The air conditioner wheezed in the background. He said: "That damn air conditioner. Has the man been?"

"He came and looked. He did something to it. He was here for only fifteen minutes or so. He was singing some sort of hymn while he worked – I heard him."

"They've all got religion."

"Well, at least they believe in something. What do air conditioning men believe in … in New York, for instance?"

He raised his bottle of beer to his lips. "The dollar. And at least that's real."

She turned up the gas under the pasta she was reheating for him. The smell of garlic was too strong for her, and she wrinkled her nose; but he liked to souse things in garlic; he always had.

"Is John travelling with you?" She tried to make the question sound casual.

"Yes. There, but he's coming back before me."

"And staying in the same hotel?"

He looked up sharply. "What is this?"

"Nothing. I was only asking …"

He smiled. "What's it with John? Do you think we share a room?"

She brushed this aside. "Of course not."

"You think he's gay, don't you?"

She shrugged. "How can you tell? I know what people say, but how can they tell? He's never said anything, has he?"

"He doesn't have to."

She wanted to get off the subject, but he had more to say.

"He's discreet, of course. People like that often are. Conventional, high-achieving background – a very prominent New Zealand family. His father's a general, I think, or an admiral – something of the sort. He's used to not giving anything away."

She did not react.

"For instance," David continued, "if he knew something, he wouldn't speak about it."

"Oh yes?" Her voice was small, and she thought he might not have heard her. But he had.

"Yes."

She had her back to him, but she felt his eyes upon her.

She stirred the pasta. It was already cooked and it would spoil if she over-heated it. But it was hard for her to turn round. "That's good."

"You know what I think?"

She struggled to keep her voice even. "What?"

He finished his beer, tilting the bottle to get the last few drops. "I think he rather likes me."

She reached for the plate she had put on the side of the stove. "Likes you? Likes you as a friend? As a colleague?"

A mocking tone crept into his voice. "Come on, Amanda. Come on."

She dished out the pasta. The odour of garlic rose from the plate, drowning the tomatoes, the onion, the slices of Italian sausage. "You mean he likes you … like that?"

He nodded. "Who knows? I've done nothing to encourage him in that view. And he knows that I'm not interested."

She put the plate in front of him at the table. She and Clover had eaten earlier, but she usually sat down and kept him company when he came in late like this. "He may not know. Or he might think that you … well, that you liked men as well as liking women."

He began his meal, spearing pieces of pasta on his fork. "I doubt it. And anyway, frankly I wouldn't care to try …"

"I'm glad to hear that."

"I'm going to have another beer."

She rose to her feet. "I'll get it."

It was while she was reaching into the fridge that he told her. "He came to see me the other day, you know. In the office. He stood in the doorway for a few seconds, as if he were hesitating. Then he came in. He said that he wanted to speak to me about something."

She was holding the bottle of cold beer. Her hand was wet. She did not turn round.

"Then he kind of clammed up. He shook his head and said it had been nothing. He said: some other time. Something like that."

She straightened up. "Your beer. Here it is."

He opened the bottle. "Poor John. It must have been something to do with his private life. I would have been perfectly happy to listen to him – he maybe doesn't have anybody else to speak to – living on his own, as he does."

She sat down.

"Mind you, it could have been something to do with the office. Jenny is being a real pain in the neck right now. She's taken it into her head that we need to change all our internal procedures. It's chronic." He went on to describe Jenny's plans and nothing more was said about John. After a few minutes, she made the excuse of going to check that the children had finished their homework. She left the kitchen and made her way along the corridor that separated the living quarters from the bedrooms. She stopped halfway, in front of a poster listing the islands of the Caribbean. She remembered how she had stood in front of it every day, with one of the children in her arms, and read out the list of names and pointed to the islands on the map. They had been taught to identify them all, from Cuba down to Grenada. Now she found herself staring at Tortola – a small circle of green in the blue of the sea. She thought, inconsequentially, of something a friend had said the other day – "Tortolans – they're the rudest people in the Caribbean, by a long chalk. They have a major attitude problem." But could one generalise like that? And people sometimes appeared rude for a reason; here and there, history had left a legacy of hatreds that could prove hard to bury.

If John had not told him already, then he would probably do so on the trip to New York. They would be together, at close quarters. He would say something when they had drunk a beer or two. But why?

The answer came to her almost immediately. Because John was jealous of her and would like to prise him away. Perhaps he thought they would separate, and then David might move in with him – temporarily, of course – but when you had to rely on scraps of comfort, then that would be consolation enough.

She lay awake that night, not getting to sleep until two in the morning. David slept well – he always had done – and did not wake up when she got out of bed to find a sleeping tablet in the bathroom. She did not like taking pills, but these ones worked, and were for emergencies.

The next morning she slept in, and by the time she woke up David had gone to work. The children were up, but Margaret had fed them and prepared them for school. They came into her bedroom to kiss her goodbye, while Margaret hovered at the door, saying that she would drive them, and then go to the supermarket to buy things they needed for the kitchen.

Amanda lay in bed in the quiet house, staring up at the

ceiling. If she had been uncertain what to do last night, now her mind was made up. She would speak to John and ask him, once again, to refrain from telling David. She would remind him that David had told her that he had clearly wanted to say something. She would shame him; she would accuse him of breaking his promise.

She dressed quickly. She knew that John was always one of the first to get into the office in the mornings; she would phone him there and arrange to meet him for coffee somewhere down near the harbour; there was a place that she knew they sometimes went to with clients.

She reached him; he sounded hesitant when he realised it was her. But he agreed to meet her for coffee an hour later.

"I can't be long," he said, as he sat down opposite her. "I have a meeting. There are some people coming in from Miami."

"I won't keep you."

He looked at her enquiringly.

"It's about the other day," she said. "When I came to see you …"

He cut her short. "We don't need to go over that ground again. I told you what my … my position was. It hasn't changed."

She raised an eyebrow. "Hasn't it?"

He frowned. "No, it hasn't. And David hasn't said anything. It's water under the bridge as far as I'm concerned."

"David said that the other day you wanted to say something to him and then changed your mind."

He seemed puzzled. "Me? I wanted to tell him something?"

She thought that his surprise was genuine. Now she was not so sure that she should have sought him out. "He told me you came into his office and said that there was something you wanted to say, and then you seemed to change your mind."

The waitress brought them coffee. He reached for his cup and half-raised it to his lips; then he put it down. "Oh yes. I remember that." He seemed relieved. "That had nothing to do with this, I assure you. Nothing at all."

She looked at him silently.

"It was an office thing," he volunteered. "Somebody had taken money from the petty cash. I had an idea who it was, but I wasn't sure. I wanted to sound David out, because this person works for him, but then I thought that it was wrong of me even to voice my suspicions. It could amount to casting an aspersion over an innocent person's character – if he was innocent, that is." He looked at her. "Which we all are, of course, until somebody unearths proof against us."

She realised that she had been holding her breath. Now she released it. "So."

"Yes, that's all there was to it."

"I'm sorry, I thought that you were going to tell him. I jumped to conclusions, I suppose."

He looked at her over the rim of his coffee cup. "So it would seem." He glanced at his watch. "I'd better dash."

She nodded. "May I say one thing – just one thing?"

"Of course."

"What I told you was absolutely true. I promise you that. I'm not having an affair with George Collins. I'm just not."

He sat quite still, looking at her. "You know something? I believe you. So even if he were to ask me, I wouldn't say anything." He paused. "Is that better?"

She reached out to take his hand, and held it briefly, squeezing it in a gesture of gratitude – and friendship. "Thank you, John."

He smiled at her, weakly. He was tired; at forty-three, he was tired. 'The problem with Cayman," he said, "is that it's too small. We all live on top of one another and spend far too much time worrying about what other people are thinking."

"You're right."

"I know I'm right. That's why I'm getting out five years from now. To the day. My forty-eighth birthday. I'll be in a position to stop work. I don't want to be an international partner. I don't want any of that. That's me off."

"Back to ..." She was not sure where he was from.

"Not back to anywhere. Somewhere new. I've been thinking of Portugal. I know people who have moved there. They bought a vineyard – which is as good a way of losing one's money as anything."

"I can see you being happy there."

He seemed to be weighing what she said.

"It's not that I see you as being unhappy here," she said hurriedly.

He smiled, and stood up. "But you know I am – you know I'm unhappy. So why say that I'm not? Is unhappiness something we're ashamed to admit to?"

She shook her head.

"To cheer me up?" he prompted.

She met his gaze. "Maybe. We don't want others to be unhappy, do we?"

He agreed. "Not really. But perhaps we should allow them their unhappiness, don't you think? Just allow it?"

"Of course." She let her gaze wander. It was bright outside, as it almost always was, with that intense Caribbean light that left no room for subtlety. It was a light that seemed to demand cheerfulness, that somehow went so well with a steel band. Just inside the door, the bored waitress answered her phone, starting an animated conversation that became louder and louder as the emotion behind it rose. *Why you think that? Why you do that?*

John caught Amanda's eye, and the glance they exchanged was eloquent. She looked away; she did not feel superior to that woman, which is what she felt the glance implied.

"She's the victim," she muttered. "She's his victim."

He shrugged. "Life," he said.

Something rose within her. "You're above all that?"

He studied her. She noticed the coldness that had appeared in his eyes. "You don't imagine that I have feelings like that?"

She back-tracked. "I'm sorry. I didn't say that. Or I didn't mean to." She hesitated. "It's just that you seem to be so detached. You seem to be so in control of yourself."

He looked at his watch. "I don't see what's wrong with self-control." He looked at her. "Do you have a problem with it?"

For a moment she wondered whether this amounted to a retraction of what he had said earlier, when he had assured her that he believed her. Was he now implying that it was a lack of self-control that had led to an involvement with George? Was that what he really believed?

She answered him quietly. "No, I don't. But there's a difference between self-control and repression, don't you think?"

Her words seemed to hit him physically, as words can do when they shock the person to whom they are addressed. It can be as if an invisible gust of wind, a wall of pressure, has had its impact. For a short while he did nothing, but then he looked at his watch, fiddling with the winder, as if to adjust it.

She immediately relented. "I shouldn't have said that."

He raised his eyes to hers. "But it may be true." He paused. "Repression may have something to do with a lack of confidence, don't you think? In fact, it probably does. But I've decided to live with it. You see, I can't find what I want to find and I know that I never will. It's different for you."

She reached out to him again. "John …"

"No, it's fine. I don't mind."

"I'm the unhappy one," she said. "It's me. Or it's both of us, maybe."

"You?"

She spoke without thinking about what she was saying. "I no longer love David."

The coldness had disappeared; the distance between them seemed to melt away. "I'm sorry to hear that."

She suddenly felt reckless. The initial unplanned admission seemed to lead quite naturally to what she went on to say. "I love somebody else. I didn't want to. Of course, falling in love with somebody is never a result of wanting to do it …"

"No, I suppose you're right."

"It just happens," she went on. "It's like finding that you have a cold. It's just there."

"You could say that." He was looking at her with interest. "Is it reciprocated?"

"What?"

"Your feelings for this other person … are they reciprocated?"

She hesitated. "I think so."

"So, do you mind my asking: who?" He immediately thought better of the question. "I'm sorry, I shouldn't ask. It's none of my business."

It did not occur to her to keep it from him now; it was too late to dissemble. "George." But then she went on. "But I'm not having an affair with him. I haven't been lying to you about that. He's … he's off-limits."

"Because he's married? That doesn't seem to stop people round here."

She smiled. "Maybe not. But we have children. Alice is in love with him and he's a good man. So put that all together and you have a fairly impossible picture."

He looked thoughtful. "I'm sorry about that."

"So whatever your situation is, John – I think I understand."

He looked at his watch again. "I really have to go. These people from Miami …"

He signalled to the waitress, who looked at him, vaguely irritated by the disturbance to her call. He stood up, which persuaded the waitress to act. He paid for them both.

"I don't think we need to have this conversation again," he said to Amanda as they went out into the light. "You needn't worry."

She felt that he was closing off two subjects: her and him.

14

The ceremony at the Prep School to mark the end of the school year took place while David was in New York. The leavers, now aged twelve or thirteen – thirteen in the case of Clover and James – were presented with a certificate bearing the school motto and a message from the Principal about embarking on the journey that was life. The Governor attended and the school band played a ragged version of "God Save the Queen"; the Governor, in a white tropical suit, stood stiffly to attention, and seemed to be interested in something that was happening on the ceiling; one or two of the younger children, fidgeting and giggling, attracted discouraging looks from the teachers. Then the choir trooped onto the stage and sang "Lord Dismiss Us, With Thy Blessing". Hymns had made little impression on Clover, but the words of this one were different, and touched her because she sensed that it was about them. "May thy children may thy children, Those whom we will see no more …" The children were sitting with their parents; Clover was with Amanda and Margaret, because David was away. Margaret knew the hymn, and reached for Clover's hand. "That's you, isn't it?" she said quietly. "Leaving your friends, saying goodbye."

Clover turned away, embarrassed; she did not want to be told how she felt. She looked around the hall, searching for James, and found him just a few rows away, seated between his parents. He was whispering something to his father, and George nodded, whispering something back. She watched them, willing him to turn his head slightly so that he would see her. I'm here, she thought. Here. I'm here.

At the end of the ceremony, the parents left, and the children returned to their classrooms. The leavers were each given a large bag in which to put the things they wanted to take away with them: the drawings, the exercise books, the pictures from the walls that the teacher said could be shared out amongst those who wanted them, as mementoes of the school.

James was in a different class, and once outside in the corridor, she lingered until she saw him emerge from his own classroom with a few other boys. They were talking about something under their breath; one gave a snigger; boys were always doing that, laughing at something crude, something physical.

She waited until the other boys were distracted before she approached him.

"Do you feel sad?" she asked.

He looked round. "Clover …"

"I mean, do you feel sad about leaving everybody? All your friends?"

He shrugged. He was smiling at her; he seemed pleased to be talking to her, and this encouraged her. "I'm really sorry to be saying goodbye to everybody," she continued.

"We'll see them in the holidays. We're not going away forever."

"No, but …"

She felt her heart beating loud within her. She could ask him; there was no reason why she could not ask him. They were meant to be friends, and you could ask a friend to your house if you wanted to.

It was as if somebody else's voice was speaking. "Do you want to come back to my place? We could have lunch there. Margaret's made one of her cakes."

He glanced at the other boys. "I don't know …"

"Please."

He hesitated, and then replied, "Yes. All right."

She felt a rush of joy. He was going to be with her. The others – Ted, these boys she did not know very well – none of them would be there; it would just be her.

Her mother was out; she had said something about a lunch for the Humane Society after the event at the school; they were always raising money for the homeless dogs shelter. Billy was with Margaret, being spoiled.

"Those dogs are rich by now," she said, as they went into the kitchen. "They raise all that money for them – just a few mangy dogs."

"It gives them something to do," said James.

"The dogs?"

"No, the parents. The old people too. They raise money for the dogs because they haven't got anything else to do."

She frowned as she thought about this. Did adults play? Or did they just talk? "Have you ever thought what it'll be like when we're old? Twenty? Thirty?"

He sat down at the kitchen table, watching her as she took Margaret's cake tin out of the cupboard. "Do you mean, will we feel the same?"

She nodded. "Yes. Will we think the same things?"

"We'll feel the same inside, maybe, but we won't think about the same things. I think you feel tired when you're that age. You run out of breath."

"When you're twenty?"

"I think that's when it starts."

She cut two slices of the lemon cake that Margaret had baked the day before, and slid each onto a plate. He picked his slice up eagerly.

"Everything's going to start to get different," she said. "From today onwards."

"Because we're going to boarding school?"

She said that this is what started it. But there would be other things.

"Such as?"

She did not have an answer. "Just things."

"I don't care," he said.

"Neither do I." But it was bravado; she did. She had lain awake the night before and fretted over what it would be like to be with a group she had never met before, sharing a room with another girl, which would be a new and confusing experience.

"How do you decide when to turn the light out?" she asked.

"When?"

"At school – when you're sharing."

He was not sure, but he thought they probably told you. "There'll be a rule. There are lots of rules. You just have to follow them."

She watched him lick the crumbs off his fingers. "Are you nervous?"

He affected nonchalance. "About going off to school? No, of course not. What's there to be nervous of?"

Everything, she thought.

He finished the last of the crumbs. "I'd better go home."

She caught her breath. "Why?"

"I don't know. I suppose I just should."

She asked him whether he would stay – just for a short while. He looked at her, and smiled. He likes me, she thought; he likes me again because he wouldn't smile like that if he didn't.

"We could have a swim."

He looked through the open kitchen door; the pool was at the back of the house, on the edge of the patio, and the water reflected the glare of the sun back into the building.

"I haven't brought my swimming trunks."

"There are some in the pool house. We keep them for visitors. Come on."

He got up reluctantly, following her to the pool house under the large sea-grape tree that dominated that end of the garden. Inside, it was dark and cool. There was a bench used for changing and a shower. The shower could not be completely shut off, and dripped slowly against the tiles beneath. There was the smell of water.

She opened a cupboard. There was a jumble of flippers and snorkels, used for the sea; a rescue ring, half eaten away by something; a long-poled net for scooping leaves from the surface of the water. The net slipped and fell onto the floor.

"The pool-men bring their own stuff," she said. "They come to clean the pool every week. The man who supervises them is almost blind now. My mother says he'll fall into a pool one of these days."

"He should stop," said James. "You shouldn't do jobs like that when you're blind."

"No, you shouldn't."

She moved the flippers, looking behind them. "There were some trunks. We had some. Maybe the pool-men took them ..."

"It doesn't matter."

She looked away. "You mean you don't need them?"

He hesitated. "I didn't mean that. I meant that I don't have to swim."

She felt her breath come quickly. "Have you ever skinny dipped?"

He did not answer for a moment, and she repeated her question. "Never?"

He laughed nervously. "Of course I have. Once at Rum Point. Off my dad's boat too."

"I dare you," she said.

"You serious?"

She felt quite calm. "Why not?"

He looked about him. "Now?"

"Yes. There's nobody around."

"And you too?"

She nodded. "Of course. I don't mind." She added, "Turn round, though. Just to begin with."

He turned his back, and she slipped out of her clothes. The polished concrete floor was cool against the soles of her feet. She felt goose-bumps on her arms, although it could not be from cold. Is that because I'm afraid? she asked herself. This was the most daring thing she had ever done, by far; and the goose-bumps came from that, obviously.

He said, "And you have to turn round too."

"Okay."

She turned round, and faced the wall. But there was a mirror, for doing your hair after the shower; her mother used it; he had not seen it, or it had not occurred to him that she could see him in it. She saw it suddenly and found herself watching him. She could not help herself. She thought: he's perfect. And she felt a lightness in her stomach that made her want to sit down, it was so overwhelming, so unexpected.

Naked now, he turned round, and immediately he saw the

mirror. Their eyes met in the glass, and she saw him blush.

"You shouldn't cheat," he mumbled. "It's cheating to look in the mirror."

She made a joke of it. "I didn't mean to. I didn't put the mirror there."

He put his hands in front of himself, to cover his nakedness. But she saw his eyes move down her own body. She did not say anything; she wanted the moment to last, but was not sure why she should want this. There was a feeling within her that she had never before experienced. She recognised it as a longing, because it was like other longings, other experiences of wanting something so much that it hurt. This hurt, she thought; it hurt and puzzled her.

He said: "I'm going to get into the pool. Are you coming too?"

She followed him. She watched him. She wanted to touch him, but she thought: I should not be thinking this. I should not. And it frightened her that it should be so strong, this confusing, odd feeling, of wanting to touch a boy and put her hands in his hair and kiss him, which is what she had sometimes dreamed of doing, and she wondered what his lips would taste like.

He entered the water cleanly, and she followed. With the protection of the water, there was no embarrassment, and they laughed, not at anything in particular, but because they were aware that something had happened, a moment had passed. He splashed her, and she responded, the water hitting him in the face and making him splutter. He swam up to her and would have ducked her head under the water, but she dived below the surface and escaped him, although his hand moved across her shoulder. He dived too, but she kicked him away; she felt her foot against his stomach. She said, "Sorry, I didn't mean to hurt you," and he said, "You didn't."

He swept back his hair, in the way she liked him to do, and then he looked up at the sun and said, "I've got to go home now."

"Don't. I don't want you to go. Can't you stay?"

"No."

He swam back to the edge of the pool and he climbed out on the curved metal ladder, and she could not help but watch him and feel again that lurch in her stomach. He ran to the pool room; she saw the water dripping down from him, and she noticed something she had been told about but never seen, and thought: *it's because of me.* She stayed where she was, and was still there in the pool when he came out, clothed, and shouted to her that he would see her again, sometime, and thanks for the cake. She whispered goodbye and then, after he had gone, climbed up the steps and ran, as he had done, to the pool room although there was nobody to see her naked. She sat down on the bench where he must have sat, for there was a puddle of water on the floor below it, and she put her head into her hands and felt herself shivering.

15

Amanda usually went to the airport to meet David when he returned from one of his trips abroad. Going to the airport was something of a ritual in George Town – the outing to the small building that served as the island's terminal where, with Caribbean informality, disembarking passengers walked past palm trees and poinsettias and could be spotted and waved to from the terrace of the coffee bar. She took Billy, but left Clover with Margaret, who liked to take her with her to the ballroom dancing academy she frequented where, if one of the instructors was free, Clover was sometimes treated to a lesson.

On the way back to the house Billy dominated the conversation, asking his father about New York and telling him a long and complicated story about an iguana that, injured by dogs, had limped into the back yard of one of his friends from school. She slipped in a few questions, about her father, whom David had visited. Her father had been widowed a few years previously and had taken up with a woman they were not sure about.

"She drags him off to exhibitions all the time," he said. "He was about to go to one when I arrived to see him. She kept looking at her watch while I was talking to him; it made me like her less than ever."

Billy said: "This iguana, see, had a big cut on the side of his head. A dog had bitten him there, I think, and you'd think that he would have died, but he hadn't, you see."

"I think she must feel frustrated. He's obviously not making up his mind."

And Billy said: "There was another iguana – not the one that had been bitten by dogs but another one. Maybe it was his brother. He had these big spikes on his back and …"

"I wish he'd come down here to see us. She discourages him, I think."

"That happens. Perhaps you need to let go." And to Billy, he said: "How big was the iguana again?"

When they reached home, he took a shower and then swam in the pool. It was hot, and the doors of the house were kept closed to keep the cool air inside; in the background, the expensive air conditioners hummed. There was a cost here to everything, she had once remarked; even to the air you breathed.

She watched him through the glass of the kitchen door. It was like watching a stranger, she thought; she could be standing in a hotel watching one of the other guests, an unknown man, swimming in the pool. He was towelling himself dry now, and then he threw the towel down on the ground, and she thought: *I'll have to pick that up.*

She went outside, taking him the ice-cold bottle of beer that she knew he would want. He took it from her without saying anything.

"Thank you," she said quietly. It was what she said to Billy, to remind him of his manners. It was what every parent said, time after time, like a gramophone record with a fault in the grooves.

He looked at her sharply. "I said thanks."

She went over to examine a plant at the edge of the patio. He followed her, beer in hand; she was aware of him behind her, but did not say anything.

"Tell me," he said. "Tell me: did you have coffee with John the other day?"

She answered without thinking. "John Galbraith? No. Why would I have coffee with John?"

He took a swig of the beer. "That's what I'm asking."

"I told you: I didn't."

She had lied instinctively, self-protectively, as people will lie to get more time.

It was as if he had not heard her answer. "It seemed odd to me, you see," he continued. "Because you never mentioned it to me."

"I didn't mention it because it didn't happen."

He looked at her in disbelief. "But it did."

She sighed. "You're picking a fight."

"No, I'm not. I'm simply asking you something."

She struggled to remain calm. "I told you. I didn't have coffee with John. I don't know why you should think I did." She paused, thinking of how rumours circulated. It was a small place; inevitably somebody had seen her and had talked about it. Why should she be in the slightest bit surprised by that?

"Whoever told you must be mistaken," she said. "Maybe it was somebody who looked like me."

"Or looked like John?"

There was an innuendo in his comment that she ignored. "People think they've seen somebody and they haven't. It happens all the time."

"It was me," he said.

This stopped her mid-movement.

He was staring at her. She noticed that he was holding the bottle of beer tightly – so tightly that his knuckles were white with the effort. For a moment she imagined that he might use it as a weapon; instinctively she moved away.

"Yes," he said. "I saw you because I had called in somewhere earlier that morning and was coming back to the office. I walked past that coffee bar near the entrance to our building. I walked right past and saw you sitting there with him."

She said nothing. She averted her eyes.

"And then," he continued, "when I was in New York, I asked John directly. I said: what were you and Amanda talking about the other day?"

It felt to her as if there were a vice around her chest.

"And do you know what?" David went on. "He said: I don't know what you're talking about. That's what he actually said. He flatly denied it. I let the matter go."

She felt a rush of relief, of gratitude. John was covering for her. He was as good as his word. "Well, there you are," she said. "You must have imagined it. Or you saw two people who looked a bit like us. The eye plays tricks, you know."

He took a step forward, bringing himself almost to the point where he was touching her. Now he spoke carefully, each word separated from the word before with a pause. "I saw you. I did *not* make a mistake. I saw you."

"You *imagined* you saw me."

"I *saw* you. I *saw* you."

She fought back. "Even if you did, then so what? So what if I have coffee with one of your friends. I know him too, remember. And anyway, are you seriously suggesting that there's something between me and John, of all people?"

"It's not that," he said. "It's why you should lie to me – which you've done recently on more than one occasion."

She tried to be insouciant. "Oh, so many occasions then …"

"The Grand Old House. You went there with somebody – I don't know who it was – but you didn't tell me. You gave an account of your evening that very specifically omitted to say anything about your being there. But you were, weren't you?"

She faltered. "The Grand Old House …"

"I didn't see you myself, but one of the girls from the office said you were there. She told me. She said: I saw your wife. I saw her yesterday. I wanted to say 'hi' to her, but she was with a man I didn't know."

"Your spies are everywhere, I see."

"Don't make light of it," he hissed. "It was another lie. It can't have been John you were with. But John's involved in some way, though I don't know how."

She felt a growing sense of desperation at being accused of doing something of which she was innocent. And yet she could assert that innocence only by confessing to something else – something that would implicate George, who was also every bit as innocent as she was. But then she thought: am I completely innocent? I entertained the possibility of an affair; I sought out George's company; I went some way down the road before I turned back.

When she spoke now, there was irritation in her voice. "I am not seeing John. If you can't understand that, then you can't understand anything."

He appeared to think for a while before responding to this. "I don't understand why you should tell me lies unless you have something to hide. And if I conclude it's an affair, then, forgive me, but what else am I expected to think?"

"But you yourself think he's gay."

He became animated. "Yes, I did think that. Not any more. I don't think he is. I asked him, you see."

She was incredulous. "And he discussed it with you?"

"John is impotent. That's the issue with him."

She was at a loss for anything to say.

David watched her. "Yes. That's quite the disclosure, isn't it?"

"Yes, I suppose it is."

"He gets fed up with people thinking that he's gay. He says that it's nothing to do with being anti-gay – which he isn't – it's to do with people making an assumption. He says that he understands how gay people might resent others treating them differently. Patronising them, maybe; pitying them. They put up with a lot."

"So he opened up to you about this to stop you reaching the wrong conclusion."

"So it would seem."

Of course it added up; it might explain the sense of disappointment that she felt somehow hung about him. But was that its effect? Did men in that position mourn for something, in the same way that a childless woman might mourn for the child she never had? Was it that important – that simple, biological matter: could it really count for so much?

David continued. "He told me when we were in New York. He became very upset when he talked about it. He said that it's been with him all his life, and it has spoiled everything – his confidence in particular. He's never had a girlfriend – never."

She had not expected that, but it made sense of the conversation she had had with him. He had said something about confidence; she tried to remember what it was, but could not.

She considered telling him the real truth now. She could do that, of course, but the problem was that the truth would sound implausible and he would be unlikely to believe it. And why should he believe her anyway, in the light of her lies? So she said, instead: "Don't you think I'm entitled to a private life?"

The question surprised him. "You mean …" He struggled to

find the words. "Are you talking about an open marriage?"

The term sounded strangely old-fashioned. She had not meant that, but now she grasped at the idea. "Yes."

He shook his head in disbelief. "Are you serious?"

"Never more." She was not; she had not thought about it until a few seconds ago.

He put down the half-empty bottle of beer. "Listen," he said. "We've fallen out of love. We both know that, don't we?"

She met his gaze now. Anger and resentment had turned to acceptance; to a form of sorrow that she was sure they now both felt.

She fought back tears. She had not cried yet for her failing marriage, and now the realisation came that she would have to do this sooner or later. "I'm so sorry, David. I didn't think this would happen, but it has."

He spoke calmly. "I'm sorry too. I don't want this to be messy."

"Of course not. Think of the children."

He picked up the bottle of beer and took a sip. "I've thought about them all the time. I'm sure you have too."

"So what shall we do?" She marvelled at the speed with which everything had been acknowledged.

They were standing outside on the patio. He looked up. Evening had descended swiftly, as it does at that latitude; an erratic flight of fruit bats dipped and swooped across the sky. "Can we stay together for the children's sake?" he asked. "Or at least keep some semblance of being together?"

"Of course. They're the main consideration." She was thinking quickly. Now that they had started to discuss their situation, the whole thing was falling into place with extraordinary rapidity. And the suggestion that came next, newly minted though it was, bore the hallmarks of something that had been worked out well in advance. "If they're going to school in Scotland, I could live there. I'll live in Edinburgh. Then we could all come out here to see you in their school holidays."

He weighed this. He had thought that she might mention the possibility of returning to the United States, which is what he did not want; he would lose the children then; lose them into the embrace of a vast country he did not understand. "I'd stay in the house here?"

"Why not? It's yours, after all."

He seemed reassured. "I'd still meet all expenses."

That was one thing he had never cavilled at; he had been financially generous to her – very financially generous – and she thanked him for it. "You've been so good about money."

He laughed. "It's what I do, after all."

"But you could have been grudging, or tight. You weren't – ever."

He said nothing about the compliment, but he reached out to touch her gently. "Friends?"

She took his hand. "Yes." She paused. "About John …"

"You don't have to."

"John saw me, seeing George. I was worried that he would misinterpret what was going on. And he did."

He caught his breath. "George Collins?"

"Yes. It didn't mean anything – or maybe it did. But we were never lovers. I enjoyed his company and … Why can't a married person have friends? Why not?"

"Don't tell me," he said quietly. "I don't want to know."

"It's not what you think." But then she said, "I feel something for George. I just do. I can't help it."

"What everyone says."

She felt that she did not have to explain. He was the cold one; he was the one who had chilled their marriage. "You're to blame too," she said. "You lost interest in me. All you ever thought about was your work, and that's still the case, I think."

"I don't think that's fair. Don't try to transfer blame. The fact remains – we're out of love."

"Which is exactly the position of an awful lot of married couples. They just exist together. Just exist." She looked at him. "Is that really what you want, David?"

He turned away. "No," he said. "And now that we've made a plan, let's not unstitch it."

"You don't plan your life just like that, without thinking a bit more about it."

"Don't you? Some people do. They make decisions on the spur of the moment. Big decisions."

There was one outstanding matter, she thought, and now she raised it. "And we each have our freedom?"

"In that sense?"

"Yes. We can fall in love with somebody else, if we want to."

He shrugged. "That's generally what happens, isn't it? People fall in love again."

It sounded so simple. But what was the point of being in love with somebody who was not free to be in love with you?

He said, "I must go and get changed."

She nodded absent-mindedly. Marriage involved little statements like that – I'm doing this; I'm doing that – little explanations to one's spouse, a running commentary on the mundane details of a life. She was free of that now; she would no longer have to explain. But still she said, "I'm going inside," and went in. She stood quite motionless in the kitchen, like somebody in a state of shock, which in a way she was. She crossed the room to the telephone. She knew George's number without looking it up, as she had made an attempt to remember it and it had lodged there, along with birthdays and key dates. The mnemonic of childhood returned: *In fourteen hundred and ninety-two, Columbus sailed the ocean blue.* Those were the last four digits of his number: 1492. It would be so easy to dial them.

16

"All right. I've told you all about me. Now it's your turn. Tell me all about yourself. Everything. I want to hear everything. Don't leave anything out."

There were just the two girls in the room, which was a small study, plainly furnished with two desks above each of which a bookcase had been attached to the wall. These bookcases had been filled with textbooks – an introduction to mathematics, physics, a French grammar – and a few personal items – a framed photograph of a dog, a lustrous conch shell; mementoes of home.

It was Katie who spoke, and she waited now for Clover's answer.

"It'd be boring to tell you everything."

'No," said Katie. "It wouldn't. I want to know. Everything. If we're sharing, I have to know. I just have to."

"I come from the Cayman Islands. Well, that's where my parents went to work and I have lived there all my life. It's home, although my mother's moving to Edinburgh now and my father is going to stay out there – for his job.

"I have one brother, Billy. He's all right, I suppose. You said you have a younger brother, so you know what I mean. He's going to school in Edinburgh and will be living with my mum. That's why she's moved, you see – to be there for Billy while he's at school.

"There was somebody back in Cayman who helped look after us. She's called Margaret. She's a brilliant cook, but she's got this husband who's really thin – you should see him – you wouldn't think he was married to somebody who was such a great cook. She's from Jamaica. Those people put a lot of hot spices in their cookery and they have this pepper that they call Scotch Bonnet. You can't actually eat it or it would burn your mouth off. You put it in a stew and then you take it out – it leaves some of the hotness behind it."

She made a gesture of completeness. "That's all."

"Come on!"

"There really isn't much more."

"What about friends? Who are your friends?"

She told her about friends at school.

"And any boys?"

She did not answer at first, and Katie had to prompt her. "I told you about Andy. You have to tell me."

"There's a boy called James."

"I love that name." Katie rolled her eyes in mock bliss. "I wish I knew somebody called James. Is he nice?"

Clover nodded. "He's the nicest boy I've ever met. You know how boys are – how they always show off? He's not like that. He's the opposite."

"He's kind?"

"Yes. He listens to you. He's easy to speak to."

"I love him already," said Katie. "Have you been out with him?"

"We went to a movie once – with some other people."

"That doesn't count. Not if there were other people. That's not a proper date."

"You didn't go out with Andy."

"I never said I did. I said I *wanted* to, but he never asked me."

"Well, James asked me to go to that movie. And he's been to my house loads of times."

Katie took time to ponder this. "He must like you."

She hesitated, and Katie seized on the hesitation. "He doesn't? That's really bad luck, Clovie. Really bad luck."

'I didn't say he didn't like me. He's just not ready. Boys are a couple of years behind us. You know that."

The conversation switched to mothers. "Mine won't leave me alone," said Katie. "She wants to interfere with everything I do – everything."

"Maybe she's unhappy," said Clover.

It had never occurred to Katie that her mother, a socialite, could be anything but in the mood for a party. "She's never unhappy," she said. "But that doesn't stop her trying to ruin *my* happiness."

"Poor you," said Clover.

She thought of Amanda in her flat in Edinburgh, which seemed so diminished after the house in the Caymans. The whole world here seemed diminished, in fact; the horizons closer, the sky lower, the narrow streets affording so little elbow room; the sea, which they could just make out in the distance from the windows of the flat, was so unlike the Caribbean that it could be a different thing altogether. Instead of being a brilliant blue, as the sea should be, it was a steely grey, cold and uninviting.

The move made it seem to Clover that their whole world had been suddenly and inexplicably turned upside down. The decision had been presented to her as a slight change of plan "just for the time being" – but she knew that it was more than that. No modern child can be unaware of divorce or of the fact that parents suddenly may decide to live apart; Clover knew this happened because there were friends at school for whom it had been the pattern of life: adults moved in with one another, moved out again, and took up with somebody else. It was what adults did. But this was something that happened to other people – like being struck by lightning or being eaten by a shark – it never happened to oneself.

The move may have been precipitate, but the truth was revealed slowly. "Daddy and I are happier, you know, if we're doing separate things. You'll understand that because you know how friends often want to do something different from what you yourself want to do. It's just the way it is."

"Yes, I suppose so."

"And if you're living with somebody you can sometimes want to have a bit more time to yourself. You must feel that sometimes – when Billy's being a nuisance. It doesn't mean that you don't like the other person any more – it's just that you feel a bit happier if you have more time to yourself."

"Maybe. But if you love the other person, won't you miss him?"

That had been more difficult for Amanda to answer. "Love changes, darling. At the beginning it's like a rocket or one of those big fireworks – you know the sort – that sends all sorts of stars shooting up all over the place, and then it dies down a bit. That happens with love. You don't necessarily stop loving somebody, but you might just decide to live in separate places so that you can have that time to yourself. That's the way it works."

She thought about this. Lying in bed on that first night in Edinburgh, a few days before she was due to be taken up to Strathearn to begin her first term at boarding school, she thought about what her mother had said about love. *It dies down.* That was what she had said: *it dies down.* Love was very important; it was something that people talked about a lot. They also sang about it – just about every song she heard was about being in love. And some of these songs, she had noticed, were unhappy.

People sang because they were in love with somebody who did not notice them nor love them back. This saddened them, and they sang songs to express the sadness.

She lay in her bed looking up at the darkened ceiling. *Am I in love?* It was a question she had never thought she would ask herself because love, she had felt, belonged to some unspecified future part of her life; it was not a question to be asked, or answered, at this stage, when she was just embarking on life.

But there was only one person she really wanted to see. It was such an unusual, unsettling feeling that she wished that she could talk to somebody about it. She was close to her mother, and they had had that earlier conversation about James, but she now felt that she could not say anything more because her mother would discourage her. There was something awkward in her parents' relations with James's mother and father – something that she could not quite put her finger on. They did not like one another, she felt, but she was not sure why this should be so.

On the day before she left for Strathearn, she sent an e-mail to Ted and asked him to pass on a message to James. She had an address for Ted, but not for James, to whom she had not had a chance to say a proper goodbye. "Please pass on this message to James – I think you have his address. Tell him to send me his e-mail address so that I can write to him. I know he's going to be starting school in England soon, but he must have an address. So please ask him to send it to me, just so that we can chat."

Ted wrote back almost immediately. "I asked James and he said that he doesn't like getting lots of e-mails as he doesn't have the time to answer them all. He says sorry, and he hopes you don't mind. He says that he'll see you in the school holidays in Cayman. Maybe."

She re-read this message several times. It occurred to her that Ted might not have spoken to James at all – Ted was quite capable of telling lies, as everybody seemed to be. He had never wanted to share James as a friend, and this was his way of thwarting her. On the other hand, he might be telling the truth. It might be that James did not like dealing with e-mail – some boys were like that – and the important thing then was that he had said that he would see her in the school holidays. That meant that he wanted to see her, and that gave her comfort.

But when the much anticipated school holidays came round for the first time, the Christmas holiday, her mother told her that they would not be returning to Cayman but would spend the time in Edinburgh. "Daddy will come. He has to be in London for a meeting, and so you'll see him here. We'll all be together as a family."

She could not hide her disappointment. "But it's so nice in Cayman at Christmas. It's the nicest time of the year."

"I know, darling. I know the weather's gorgeous …"

"Which it isn't here – not at Christmas. It'll be cold."

"Of course it'll be cold. It might even snow. Imagine that – a Christmas with snow lying about. Imagine how you'll like that."

There was no persuading her mother, who eventually revealed that the decision had been taken by David. "Your father wanted it this way. I suggested that it would be good for us all to get a bit of sun, but he wouldn't shift. I'm sorry, darling, but that's the way it's going to have to be."

For the first few days, having her father in the house seemed to her to be almost like having a guest, an ill-at-ease stranger. He spent more time with Billy than with her, taking him out on expeditions that ended with the boy being spoiled with the purchase of yet another expensive present.

"He likes Billy more than he likes me," she said to her mother.

"That isn't true. You mustn't think that, darling. Daddy likes you both exactly the same. And the same goes for me. You're both the most precious things we have in this world."

"Really?"

"Yes, of course."

"Then why don't we go back to the way it was before? Why don't we go home?"

"To Cayman?"

"Yes, that's home, isn't it? That's where we grew up."

Amanda tried to explain. "But remember that you're not Caymanian. You're half Scottish and half American. That makes you different from real Caymanians. They don't have somewhere else to go back to."

"They aren't any different from me. Just because their parents ..."

"That's exactly what makes the difference, darling. Parents. You get to be something because your parents are something. That's the way the world works."

"So I have to live somewhere I don't want to be just because you come from somewhere else?"

This was answered with a nod: the injustices of the world – the rules and red tape – could be difficult to explain to a child.

"And James?" she asked.

Her mother made a gesture of acceptance. "It's different for him, I think. His father has Caymanian status and I believe that James has that too. It's because his father is a doctor. You know all about that, don't you? The right to stay there? He can live there for the rest of his life if he wants."

"That's unfair."

"Yes, it is. You're right – it's very unfair." Amanda paused. "Have you heard from him? I wonder how he's getting on at his new school."

"I haven't heard."

"You could write to him. Send him an e-mail."

She looked away. "I tried to. I sent my address to Ted and asked him to pass it on to James. But then Ted said that James didn't want to write to me."

Amanda glanced at her daughter; the pain of love at that age was so intense – one might easily forget just how bad it could be. It would be transient, of course, but children did not know that; what they felt, she had heard, they thought they would feel forever. "Darling, that can happen. People can make new friends. They don't mean to upset us when they do that – it's just the way that things work out."

"I'd never say I wouldn't write to a friend," said Clover.

"I'm sure you wouldn't."

"I hate him."

That meant, Amanda knew, that she loved him. She had hated somebody once because she loved him; she remembered. Yet there would have to be a parental reproach. "No, you don't hate him. You mustn't hate somebody else because they drift away from you. That's very unkind."

Clover went to her room. She lay down on the bed and stared out of the window at the December sky. It was getting dark already, and it was only three in the afternoon. Everything had changed. She had been happy at home with the light and the sun, and now suddenly she had been taken to a world of muted shades and misty light and silences. She thought of James. If only she could see him, then all this would be bearable; he would be like the sun, his presence dispelling the cold, the damp air, the pervading grey.

She took a piece of paper and wrote on it. *I love James. I love James. I said that I hated him, but that's not true. I said I hated him because I love him so much. I love him and have always loved him. Always.* The writing of these words gave her a curious feeling of relief. It was as if she had made a confession to herself – admitting something that she had been afraid to admit but that, now acknowledged, was made much easier to bear, as a secret when shared with another is deprived of its power to trouble or to shame.

17

A pattern became established. Although there was talk of their making trips to Cayman, a reason was always found as to why it would not work. David would be away on business, or there were workmen renovating the house, or there had been an invitation to spend a few weeks in France and they could not turn this down without giving offence.

"We're never going to go back, are we?" Clover said to her mother. "And you don't want to, do you?"

"I'd love to, darling. And we will – some day. It's just that there's so much going on here, and Daddy is in the UK so often that it makes more sense for us all to be together in Scotland, or even in France. It really does."

"I want to go back to George Town. It's not the same here or in France. I want to see our house again. I want to swim at Smith's Cove. I want to do the things we used to do."

"All in good time. We'll go some day."

"Billy's even forgetting what it was like. He thinks he's Scottish now."

"Well he is, in a way. As are you. Half of you."

But in the year she turned sixteen, they went to Cayman for a month, a week being added to the three-week break the school allowed over Christmas. Amanda told Clover of the trip at the beginning of October, and the intervening months were spent in a state of eager anticipation. Three years had elapsed since they had left George Town, during which time she had settled into and accepted her new existence. There was no shortage of new friends – Strathearn was a friendly school and strong bonds were formed with her new classmates. There were boys she liked, one in particular – a studious boy from Glasgow whose passion was ornithology. He painted birds and had a collection of feathers and bird eggs. He seemed a lonely boy, and they slipped into a comfortable friendship that was, from her point of view, a long way off romance. He sent her a Valentine card one year, slipped unseen into her French dictionary, and although it was anonymous she could tell it was from him because it had a picture of a bird perching on a red heart, and he was the only boy in the school who would have chosen a card like that. She was flattered, but these cards were not something to become excited about. There was only one Valentine card that she really wanted to receive and of course it never came.

David sent her a message. "I can't wait to have you all back home," he wrote. "You and Billy and Mummy; we'll have a great time together. And you'll be able to catch up with all your old friends, which I expect you're really looking forward to. Counting the days now!"

She wrote back to him: "I know that it's soon now because the dreams I'm having are all back in Cayman – it's as if I was already there. I think this is a sign, don't you?"

He replied: "Of course it is."

The days before they left passed slowly. She made a list of things she would need to take – swimming costume, sunblock, clothes for parties. They were going to what had remained a family home in spite of her parents' separation, but she knew that everything that she had left there would be the possessions of childhood and nothing would fit her any more.

"Your room's still here," her father had written. "And it's exactly the same as it always was."

Yes, she thought; but I'm not the same. And that led her to

wonder whether James would have changed. She had looked at his Facebook page, cautiously, as if trespassing, but he did not seem to bother very much with it and there were only a few out-of-date photographs. She wondered what he would look like now; it was only three years and people did not change all that much in three years; or did they? He had still been a boy when she had seen him last, and now, at sixteen, he could look quite different. Boys changed; they became thicker and coarser. The fact that they had to shave changed everything about their faces, it seemed to her; or so it seemed with the boys at school. Some of them did not use electric razors and came to class in the morning with cuts on their chin or on their neck; she shivered at that; she hated to think of how people dragged razors across their skin that could so easily slip and slice into it and … It did not bear thinking about.

She could not imagine James doing that. His skin was smooth, and like the colour of light honey, as he tanned so easily; that was how she remembered him, anyway. She was careful about the sun because with her colouring her skin could turn red and itch. She closed her eyes. In a day or two she would be seeing him, talking to him, and everything would go back to the way it was when it had just been the two of them; before Ted started to get him involved in things that excluded her; before something happened between her mother and his and he started talking about seeing her less. They would go back to that time. That would happen; she was sure of it.

They caught a plane from Edinburgh to London, and then boarded the flight to Grand Cayman via Nassau. On the ground in the Bahamas, when all the Cayman passengers had to stay on board, she looked out of the window into the Caribbean glare, watching a man driving a small airport truck, a shepherd of great jets, fussing about on some errand opaque to others. The cleaners came on in a bustle of energy, removing the detritus left by the passengers who had disembarked in Nassau; she heard the patois of their conversation and found that she understood; she had not heard it for a long time, but she understood it, and realised that this was the language of home. She wanted to join in, but did not, as the cleaners looked straight through the passengers, who were simply not there for them; they were too rich, too alien. She wanted to say something that would tell them that this did not apply to her; that she was Caymanian and she knew what it was like. But she did not.

She turned to her mother in the seat beside her.

"Are you looking forward to getting there?"

Amanda smiled. "Of course."

"To seeing Daddy?"

"What?"

"Looking forward to seeing Daddy?"

"Of course I am."

She was silent. "Can't you get together again?"

Amanda reached out and took her hand. "Sometimes these things happen. People find it easier to live apart."

"Because they don't like each other any more?"

Amanda hesitated. "Sometimes it's like that. But that's not really what it's like between Daddy and me. Not really."

Clover took her hand away. "I wish you would. I just wish you would."

Amanda's gaze moved to the window. A young man was driving away a refuelling truck, describing an arc across the shimmering concrete; another, wearing earmuffs against the whine of the engines, was signalling to their pilot, looking up at the cockpit as he did so. The cleaners had vanished as quickly as they came, dragging behind them the bags of litter like sacks of loot.

"Would you like me to try?"

Amanda was not sure why she said this; it had not occurred to her that the subject would come up, and she had not intended to raise it, but now she had asked her daughter whether she would like her to mend her relationship with David and Clover was going to say yes.

"Please try."

"I will." Again the words had come out without being planned, like an off-hand agreement to do something minor. But this was not minor.

"Good."

Beside Clover, Billy struggled with sleep; he had stayed awake the entire previous night – out of excitement – and now it was catching up with him. Clover tucked him up in his airline blanket; the plane's ventilation system breathed cool air upon her; she felt a welling of joy: they were going home; her mother and father would be together again, which is what she had always wanted; things lost were to be returned to her, made safe, secured.

Amanda could tell that David was nervous. He had a way of speaking when he was unsure of himself – a clipped, guarded form of speech that she had noticed before and that she had put down to the tightening of muscles that went with insecurity. It was the vocal equivalent, she thought, of sweaty palms or a thumping heart.

They had seen him on the observation terrace – standing slightly apart from a family group of Jamaicans excited at an imminent reunion. The Jamaicans waved madly, flourishing tiny Jamaican national flags, the children issuing whoops of delight; David stood stiffly, but waved enthusiastically to the children when he saw them.

"There he is!" shouted Billy. "See him, Ma? See him?"

She raised her eyes against the glare. It was early evening and the light was gentler, but it was so much brighter than in Scotland. She had forgotten just how strong it could be, this Caribbean light; how it could penetrate. Scotland, with its attenuated light, soft at the edges, allowed one to hide; to conceal, if one wanted to do so; to live in ambiguity.

She felt the warm air on her skin, and shivered. The touch of the air was what had struck her most forcibly all those years ago when she had first come here. She used to go out at night, out from the air-conditioned cocoon of their bedroom, and stand in the darkness with the night air about her like a mantle. The air clothed you here. It was like swimming. It was like that.

They moved through immigration quickly. In the baggage hall, the luggage carousel seemed tiny – a toy so small that it could have been operated by clockwork. It was silent when they went through, but about ten minutes later burst into life and started to bring suitcases. Theirs were out early, and placed on a cart that Billy had retrieved. She led them through the customs area and into the hall where David, having come down from the observation deck, was now standing. Billy ran forward and embraced his father, who lifted him up briefly before turning to Clover and kissing her on both cheeks. Then he turned to his wife.

The nervous voice: "You made it."

She nodded. "Yes. Here we are."

He took a hesitant step towards her. "Thanks. Thank you so much."

She was not sure what she had expected, but somehow she had not imagined that he would thank her.

"Margaret wanted to come," he continued. "But she couldn't."

"Something on at the church?"

He laughed, but his voice still sounded strained. "How did you guess?"

"Things don't change," she said. And she thought: but they do.

In the car he seemed to relax. Billy, delighted to discover that he recognised everything, revelled in pointing out landmarks. 'There's that tower – that radio thing. See, I remember. And there's that place that sells fishing stuff. Remember that? Remember, we went there once?"

David said, "Of course I remember." Then he added, "You're talking like a Scotsman, Billy."

"I'm not. I talk the same as everybody else."

"And everybody else around you is Scottish these days."

"Maybe."

And from Clover: "He talks too much, don't you, Billy?"

They swerved to avoid a car that had failed to signal.

"Home," Amanda muttered.

Clover would have stayed up, but she too was tired and was in bed by half past eight. Billy had managed a swim before he had fallen asleep at the table, and was helped to bed by his father. David had been tactful and had asked Margaret to prepare a separate room for Amanda at the back of the house. "You'll be all right there?" he had asked. "Margaret went out of her way to make things comfortable."

In the Caribbean winter, air conditioning was unnecessary, but Margaret had left it on at high pitch, making the room feel like a walk-in fridge. David had gestured to the thermostat and rolled his eyes. She said: "Yes. Down. If you've lived without it for years …"

"In Scotland? I suppose so."

She shook her head. "No, that's not what I meant. I meant Margaret. In Jamaica they wouldn't have had it – not at home. It would have been an impossible luxury – something dreamed of."

"And then you get it …"

"And you think you've arrived in heaven."

He smiled at her. "It's the same with food. I was reading somewhere or other …"

"*The Economist.*"

He laughed. "I do read other things. Occasionally."

She bit her tongue. She did not want to start off on the wrong foot. "Of course. Sorry. I didn't mean it like that."

He had not taken offence. "It probably was in *The Economist.* Anyway, it was about average weight in Germany. It goes up and down, apparently – just like everywhere else. But what they were saying was that in the post-war years, once their economic miracle got going, they became heavier and heavier, because they remembered when they did not have enough to eat and made up for it."

"Pigging out. Insecurity does that."

"Yes." He paused. "I've prepared something for dinner, if you've got an appetite … They keep feeding you on planes. I suppose it keeps you busy and stops people asking for things all the time."

She was hungry; she had not eaten much on the plane.

"I'm quite the cook these days," he said. "Not that I'm boasting. It's just that necessity is the mother of invention."

"I'm sorry."

He smiled. "Oh, I don't say that out of self-pity. I actually rather like it. If you look in the kitchen you'll see all my books. Delia. Jamie. All those people."

"I'm impressed."

He moved towards the door. "Come through when you've unpacked. I only have to heat it up."

Standing in the doorway, for a moment it seemed that he was going to say something else, but he did not. She looked at him expectantly, and it seemed to her that in their exchange of glances, at one time both uncertain and regretful, was the whole history of what had happened between them.

She unpacked, throwing her clothes into a drawer that she now remembered clearing, years earlier, for visitors; little thinking then that she would be a visitor in her own house. That was the most painful thing about separation, she felt: the ending of the very small things, the ordinary sharing, the unspoken reliance; removing one's toothbrush from the bathroom was as big a step, in a way, as making an appointment with the divorce lawyer.

She went into the bathroom that led off the bedroom. There was a slight smell of mustiness about it – inevitable in that climate, when towels became fusty within hours of going on the rail. But he had put a small bag of lavender on a dish, and she picked this up and smelled it, holding the muslin to her cheek. He had remembered that she loved lavender, and the thought that he had done this, had bothered himself, touched her.

She had thought about it before, of course; had entertained the possibility that she could fall in love with him again – as suddenly, perhaps, as she had fallen out of love with him. People did that, sometimes going to the extent of remarrying the person whom they had already divorced. She had met a couple like that – an elderly couple from Savanna who spent several months of each year in Cayman; he had divorced her in order to go off with a younger woman. The younger woman had treated him badly, leaving him for a youthful band instructor. He had waited a few months and then gone round to see her to propose marriage again, and she had said yes; an example of forgiveness, she had decided, when it would have been so much easier to crow, to enjoy the *Schadenfreude* that such a situation could provoke.

She looked in the bathroom mirror. What exactly was one entitled to expect from life? Romance that could last a lifetime, or, at best, the comfort of friendship with a chosen person? Had she been naïve, she wondered, to imagine that she should have remained in love with David rather than just to have lived with him in reasonable comity? Husbands and wives did not stare fondly into one another's eyes; that required mystery and a sense of wonderment at the other, which surely could not last very long. And she knew – as everybody did – that you had to accept that marriage could not be a fairy story, that you could not go through life feeling as if you have just had a glass of champagne, that all you could hope for was a sort of unchallenging companionship – an understanding not to judge each other too harshly.

Yet even that required a form of belief in the other, and that could be so quickly ruined by the wrong words, by an expressed doubt, an act of disloyalty, that would weaken the pact that you both wanted to exist. It was rather like saying that you do not believe in God; God can be a fine pretence, can give all the comfort that you need, until you doubt his presence; and with that you find that he is indeed not there.

She turned away from the mirror. She would try.

She started to leave the room, but stopped. She closed her eyes. Standing below the air conditioning vent, the cool air blew directly on her skin. And she thought: insecurity. He had brought it up when they had been talking about over-eating but now she was going over it in her mind and realising that if she went back to David it might just be because she felt at some subconscious level that this was where her best chance of security lay. She needed him because he had the money and paid for everything.

She opened her eyes again and started to make her way to the kitchen, where she heard the sounds of his preparing whatever it was he was heating up for her.

"Bouillabaisse," he announced. "Made with red snapper."

"And …"

"And conch."

She raised a hand to her lips in a gesture of gastronomic anticipation. She did not carry it through, as she felt the tears well in her eyes. How stupid of me to cry, she thought; how stupid.

"Onions," she stuttered.

But he knew that it was not the onions that she could see he had been cutting that were making her cry, but memories. He put an arm around her; and this was the first proper touch of him for years.

"Start again?"

She was unprepared for this. The move, she had thought, would come from her, not from him, and now she felt gratitude, sheer gratitude, that he had chosen to make it so easy for her. She moved against him, into his embrace. Three years, she thought, of pointless misunderstanding and separation are coming to an end in a simple touch. There had been no elaborate discussion, no rehearsal of pros and cons, and she felt that she was falling into this decision without thinking things through. But she had had enough; she had had enough of loneliness; as he had, too, she imagined.

He kissed her, and she wondered whether she really still liked it. She remembered what a friend had said to her at high school, all those years ago: *if you wouldn't use a boy's toothbrush – and you wouldn't, would you? – then why kiss him?* The things people say can ruin the things we would otherwise like to do, and kissing – or the prospect of kissing – had never seemed the same to her after that. She had forgotten what it was like to be this close to him; it was familiar and yet unfamiliar; she had become used to his separateness and had not given thought to the physical. *Perhaps I have shrivelled within me. Perhaps I can't.* "Tonight?" he said. "Or you can wait if you like. You mustn't feel under pressure."

She said that this was not the way she felt. "I feel so silly crying like this. This was not the way it was meant to be."

"But it is," he said.

His embrace turned into a playful hug, and then they broke apart, each as surprised as the other by what had happened. "Are they both asleep?" he asked, nodding in the direction of the bedrooms along the corridor.

She said she thought they were.

"Clover's very excited," he said.

She nodded. "There's a reason for that."

He looked at her enquiringly.

"She wants to see that boy," she said. She looked at him hesitantly. "James. He's the reason."

"Ah."

"Yes. I fear she's in for a disappointment. These teenage romances ... Particularly one-sided ones."

"Poor girl."

"We want to protect them, don't we? We want to protect them from the pain that we know is coming their way, but what can one do?"

He shrugged. "We can warn them. We can tell them the truth."

"That won't work," she said. "You think you know what the truth is at sixteen. All other versions of it are wrong."

"Just like us?"

"Yes. Just like we did at that age."

He sighed. "My little girl ... thinking about other men."

She laughed, and she realised that this was the first time she had laughed in his company for more than three years. He seemed to sense this too, and he grinned at her. She thought: he's changed, and of course I can fall in love with him again, or at least fall in friendship, if there is such a thing.

18

Clover saw Ted before she saw James. She had gone with her mother to the supermarket – an everyday trip but one that, after three years' interruption, was like performing once more an important ritual of childhood. It was exactly the same as she remembered it – the car park with its hotly contested shady spots; the line of shopping carts along the front of the building; the cool exhaled breath of the air conditioning as the automatic doors parted to admit you. The smell was familiar too: the ripe, sweet smell of the fruit at the entrance, and then the piquant notes from the trays of ready-made dishes. The man at the fish counter was the same man whom she had last seen standing there three years ago; his white straw hat at the same angle and the apron with his embroidered name and the printed picture of a jumping marlin. The same tired woman was spraying water over the salad vegetables and she glanced at Clover and then looked at her again before deciding that she recognised her, and nodded.

Ted was standing at the section where magazines were displayed. He was reading something about cars and he looked up and smiled broadly at Clover.

"Clove," he said. "It's you, isn't it?"

"Yes, me."

He put the magazine down. "It's great to see you."

"And you."

"I mean it," he said.

"I know you do."

They looked at one another awkwardly before she broke the ice. "I'm here with my mother. Shop, shop, shop."

"Me too."

She looked over her shoulder. "We could go and have a coffee round the corner. They're going to take ages."

"Yes, they always do."

In the coffee bar, the awkwardness that Ted had shown seemed to melt away. He told her about the school he was at – an international school in Wales – and asked her about Strathearn.

"You haven't changed," he said.

"Nor you." That was not true, she thought, but she said it nonetheless. Ted had changed; his face was thinner, she thought, and that slightly puppyish look he had at twelve was no longer there.

"But I hope I have," he said.

"Then you have."

Their order of coffee arrived.

"What are you going to do?" he asked.

"Now?"

"No. While you're here. For the next two weeks."

'Three." She paused. He was watching her. "Nothing much. Chill, I suppose."

"There's going to be a party."

She caught her breath, but tried not to look interested. "It's that time of year."

"James is having one."

He was watching for her reaction, and she could not help herself blushing. He'll be able to tell, she thought.

"Yes?"

"Yes, the day after tomorrow." Ted paused. "Would you like to come?"

She shrugged. "I don't know. He hasn't invited me."

"Oh, that doesn't matter. Nobody's being invited as such. All his friends can come."

"I'll have to think."

Ted sipped at his coffee. "I hate this stuff," he said. "I've never liked coffee. I only drink it because everybody else does."

She stared at him. "You don't have to be the same as everybody else."

He wiped cappuccino foam from his lips. "I know."

"Just be yourself. It's easier."

"Yeah, sure. Is that what you do?"

She did not answer.

"You like him, don't you?"

She affected ignorance. "Who?"

"James."

"He's all right."

Ted smiled. "No, it's more than that. You really like him, don't you?"

She turned the questioning back to him. "Well, what about you? You like him, too. You really like him."

He stiffened. "He's a friend. I like my friends."

"But some more than others."

"Sure. Who doesn't?"

He was watching her warily. She had strayed into something she had not expected, and her instinct was to move away. "I might come to the party," she said. "Will you tell him?"

"What?"

"That I'm coming."

He shrugged. "It'll be fine. I don't need to tell him … but I will, if you like." He paused, as if weighing up whether to continue. "By the way, you know how people can't stand other people?"

She said nothing. Was he going to say that James could not stand her?

"Your mother," he went on. "Your mother and James's mother. Don't go there."

She looked at him wide-eyed. "What do you mean?"

He seemed to be enjoying himself now. "You remember years ago? You remember how when we were kids we played at being detectives, or whatever. We took photographs at the tennis club."

"Sort of," she said. "It wasn't my idea – it was James's. He liked to do that sort of thing."

"Maybe, but he took them of your mother talking to his dad. And he made some sort of note about their meeting one another. Kids' stuff."

She remained silent.

"James's mother found them – the photographs. She thought that it showed that your mother and James's father were … you know … seeing one another."

She felt a sudden coldness within her. "Oh."

"James told me," Ted continued. "He said that his folks had a major row. Big time."

She could only think to say that it was not true.

"I know," said Ted. "Adults get it seriously wrong sometimes. But the point is that she hates your mother."

Clover struggled to control herself. "I don't care." She did.

"I don't think she hates you, though," said Ted. "What your mother does has nothing to do with you."

"She didn't do anything."

"I'm not saying she did. All I'm saying is that if she did something, then it wouldn't be your fault. You see the difference?"

She nodded. She felt miserable.

"James doesn't hold it against you," Ted went on. "He's cool with what happened. I suppose he's more embarrassed than anything." He paused. "He likes you, you know."

She struggled to control herself. She wanted to ask him what James had said; she wanted to hear the exact words. But she did not want Ted to know how desperately she wanted this knowledge.

"I'm not saying that he's *keen* on you," Ted said. "Not in *that* way."

She bit her lip. She tried to laugh. "I didn't think you meant that."

"He's got a girlfriend, you see."

Now she lost the battle to remain aloof, and Ted noticed. "I can tell you're upset," he said. "Sorry about that. It must be tough if you're really keen on somebody … and they don't notice you."

She tried to look scornful. "I'm not *really keen* on anybody. I don't care."

He looked unbelieving. "Don't you? You don't have to pretend with me, Clove. Remember, we've known one another since we were six, or whatever."

She looked at her watch. "I have to go." But then she added, "Who is she anyway – this girlfriend?" She stumbled on the word *girlfriend*, and had to repeat it. Ted noticed; she could tell by the way he looked away in embarrassment.

"She's called Laura," he said. He turned back to face her. "I can't stand her myself. He's only known her since the summer."

"You don't like her?"

"Of course not …" He checked himself, but she wondered why he had said *of course*.

"Why not? Why don't you like her, Ted?"

He shrugged. "You can't like everybody. You like some people, and you don't like others. It's a matter of ..."

"Chemistry?"

"Yeah, sure. Chemistry comes into it." He played with the handle of his coffee cup. "Chemistry's important, but there are other things. The things people say, for instance. Their attitude. She's keen on him – you can tell."

She tried to keep her voice level. "How?"

"She's all over him – know what I mean? She looks at him in a really intense way. Like this." He glared at Clover. "See? What do you call that?"

"I don't know."

"It's *the* look. That's what they call it. *The* look. You can always tell."

There was a straw to be clutched at. She heard her friend at school: *if you're keen on a boy, never show it – it's the quickest way of scaring them.* "That sort of look can put people off. Maybe he doesn't like it. She could be much keener on him than he is on her."

Ted was doubtful. "I think he likes her – at least that's the impression I got when he spoke to me. And when I've seen them together." He seemed to consider something. "But then you know how kind he is – he's always kind to people, isn't he?"

Yes, it was why she liked him; or one of the reasons for the way she felt: his kindness.

"So maybe he's just being kind to her?" But then Ted seemed to reject his own suggestion. "No, I don't think so. I think she's managed to get him to like her. And then there's the way she is. She's really hot. You can tell. I think he likes all that."

She stared at him. She hated hearing that, and something

made her feel that Ted did not like it either, although he was the one who said it.

"Why's she here?" she asked. People came and went in Cayman; perhaps she would not last.

"Her folks. Her dad has a job here. He's with one of the American banks, but they're Canadians themselves. She's at school in Vancouver. They have different holidays from British schools, but the summer holidays are more or less the same."

She listened to this carefully, trying to envisage Laura. "Are you sure? How do you know she's his actual girlfriend?"

"Because he told me."

"He said he was seeing her?"

Ted smirked. "More than that. He said ..."

She cut him short by standing up. "I have to get back."

"Me too. But what about the party? You can come with me if you like."

She almost said that she had no interest in going to the party – that she didn't care about James. But those were not the words that came. Instead, she nodded, and said: "All right."

They walked back to the supermarket, to meet their mothers. She separated from him at the entrance, saying goodbye without letting him see how upset she was. She felt that he probably knew, anyway, but somehow she wanted to salvage her dignity by not revealing the despair that now engulfed her like a sea-fog, as cold, as dispiriting. He could not have a girlfriend because he belonged to her. She should be his girlfriend, not some girl from Vancouver who had only just met him.

When Amanda saw her, she could tell that something was amiss. "Is it Ted?" she asked. "Did Ted do something to upset you?"

She shook her head. "He didn't."

"You look as if you're about to cry."

She turned away. "I'm not. Don't be ridiculous."

"And you should stop being so moody."

She said nothing. Her mother could not possibly understand. She was an ice maiden when it came to these things; she had no idea, none at all, about how it felt when the only boy you could ever love was seeing some Canadian girl and telling Ted about it. They were standing at the supermarket check-out now, and the woman behind the till was looking expectantly at her mother, waiting for her to unload the cart. The woman had a dull, passive look to her, and behind her, ready to pack the purchases, stood a boy with a scowl. Clover looked through the plate-glass window behind them, out into the supermarket car park; a large white vehicle, a luxury SUV, was pulling up at the kerb. She watched as a young couple got out, and said something to one another, laughed briefly, and then went back to looking bored. That's the trouble, she thought: everybody here is bored. She did not want that. She wanted something different, and that, she knew, was James. I want him more than anything I've ever wanted. I want to be with him. I want to feel him beside me. I want to be far away from everybody else, just with him. I want him to whisper to me and kiss me and tell me all his secrets and that he thinks of me all the time. That's what I want, and that's what's going to happen – it really is. It will happen if I want it hard enough.

19

"There," said Billy, pointing to a spot where the land jutted out into the sea. "That's the place. You can put everything down there and then we can swim."

Amanda had suggested a picnic, and they had agreed – Billy more enthusiastically than his sister. She had said initially that she wanted to stay at home, having things to do. Amanda had said, "To mope?"

"No. Things to do."

"Then do them after our picnic – there'll be plenty of time."

It was a place they had often visited – a place where the mangrove met a cluster of sea-grape trees and where there was enough sand to make for a small swimming beach. The beach gave way to rock formations on either side through which the sea was making slow ingress, wearing away at the basalt to produce strange indentations and incipient caves. When an onshore wind whipped up waves, the movement of the sea, though dissipated here by the protective ring of reef a mile or so further out, was sufficient to produce the occasional plume of spray from a blowhole, shooting up like a displaced ornamental fountain. As a young girl, Clover had been fascinated by this, and had been prepared to sit for hours on end, under Margaret's watching eye, waiting for the sudden eruption of white.

"Don't dive," warned Amanda, as Billy rushed to the edge of the water. "Remember what happened to that boy ..."

Billy stopped in his tracks. "Timmy ..."

"Yes, Timmy. He was lucky not to have been much more badly hurt."

Billy stared at the water. "He was knocked out, wasn't he?"

"Concussed – not quite knocked out. But it could have been much worse."

Clover joined in: "You shouldn't dive into water if you don't know exactly how deep it is."

"Your sister's right," said Amanda. "Listen to her."

"He never does," said Clover.

While the boy waded into the water, Clover and her mother unpacked the bag of picnic provisions they had brought with them. There was a flask of iced juice, and Amanda poured some for her daughter. Clover took it, drained the glass, and then lay back on the picnic rug and looked up at the sky.

"Happy to be here?" asked Amanda.

"Yes."

Amanda lay back too. "I love looking at this sky. You can't lie back in Scotland and stare at the sky."

"It would rain on you."

"Yes."

Flat out on the sand, Amanda turned her head to look at her daughter. She was an attractive girl – still obviously a teenager, but getting to the point where the adult butterfly finally emerged, where all vestiges of the vulnerability and softness of the child gave way to the grown young woman. "Happy?" she asked.

"I've already told you. Yes."

Amanda persisted. "Not just to be here, but happy in … in general. With life?"

"Yes. Of course."

"I wanted to talk to you."

Clover was still staring at the sky. "Well, we're talking, aren't we?"

"About me and Daddy."

This was greeted with silence. Above them, a high-flying jet curved a line of white across the sky.

"You see," said Amanda, "I have some rather good news for you. Or I think you'll find it good news."

There was little reaction.

"You're listening to me, I hope. You aren't going to sleep, are you?"

This brought a muttered response. "No, I'm not."

"Daddy and I are going to live together again. We've talked it through. We're getting on better and we … well, both of us have been lonely. You understand that, don't you?"

She saw her daughter stiffen. She continued to lie still, but the effect had been immediate.

"Yes, I understand. I'm a bit surprised, though."

"It's a surprise for me, too. So I'll go back to Scotland, but only to close up the flat. Then I'll come back home. Billy will go back to the Prep." She was aware of the fact that she said *home*. There had been a change, as slow, in human terms, as the erosive action of the sea on the rock: home was no longer New York, or America; it had become this place in the middle of nowhere, under a familiar, but still alien flag.

"So everything will go back to how it used to be." She paused, and reached to the flask to pour more juice. "I hope you're pleased."

Clover had raised herself onto an elbow and was looking at her mother. She was smiling. "I'm really pleased, Mum. I'm really pleased."

"Good. Then give me a kiss."

Clover leaned forward and kissed her mother on the cheek. She wanted to cry, and the tears now came, sobs, almost painful in their intensity.

"Darling, you mustn't cry …"

She struggled with the words. "It's because … because I'm so pleased."

"I'm glad."

Clover wiped at her eyes. "And Billy? Does he know?"

"I'll tell him later – after his swim. Both of us – we can both tell him. Not that he'll pay much attention."

Clover shook her head in disagreement. "He misses Dad. Surely you've noticed that."

It was a reproach, and Amanda tried to explain herself. "Yes, you're right. I suppose I was just thinking how boys don't feel so intensely about these things."

This caught Clover's attention. "They don't?"

"Well, it's a bit of a generalisation, of course, but these generalisations are often true. Or at least, I think they are. Boys – men too – are more interested in the outside world than the inside world."

"The inside world?"

"How we feel. Of course there are plenty of men who feel these things, but generally speaking they're too busy *doing* things to ask themselves how they feel about them. That's why it sometimes seems to us that they don't care about people's emotions."

"Because they're selfish?"

"Not selfish – it's more a question of indifference."

"What exactly is indifference?"

Amanda glanced across the beach to where Billy was examining something washed up by the waves – a cuttlefish, she thought. "Indifference is not worrying about others. And that may be because you don't know what they're thinking, or because you know and don't care."

"Indifference," muttered Clover, as if savouring the new word, like a new taste, experienced for the first time.

Amanda glanced at her. We let our children grow up under our noses without talking to them about these things; now she was. "Which is one of the worst things you can experience."

Clover frowned. "Why?"

"Because when we want somebody to notice us and they don't, there's a particular sort of pain involved." She paused. Billy had picked up something else – an abandoned sandal – and was waving his discovery at them. "Put it down, Billy."

"He picks everything up," said Clover. "The other day I saw him pick up a handkerchief somebody had dropped. Think of the germs."

"We need a certain number of germs – just to keep our immune systems in trim."

Clover was not convinced. "Yuck." She was looking up at the sky again; but it was indifference that was on her mind. "You were saying ..."

Amanda hesitated. She knew what her daughter was going through, and this discussion of indifference went to the heart of it. "We all want to be loved, you know. We want that rather badly."

Clover said nothing.

"And so," Amanda continued, "that's why indifference can be so painful. We may decide that we want to be loved by a particular person – and we can't really control who that will be – and if they don't love us, if they take no notice of us, we hurt. It's the way we're made, I suppose. It just is."

Clover propped herself up on an arm and stared at her mother. "Why are you saying all this?"

Amanda took a deep breath. "I'm saying it, darling, because I think that's what you may be feeling. I think you're very keen on a boy whom you haven't seen for the last three years and who is probably rather different from when you saw him last."

"He isn't," muttered Clover.

"Have you seen him? You haven't, have you?"

"I saw Ted. He told me."

Amanda smiled. "Maybe. Maybe. But the point is that you don't really know whether you're going to be able to resume the friendship you had. And you don't really know how James feels, do you?" She reached out and took Clover's hand. She felt the sand upon it; the fine white grains that would cling to your skin, like face-powder, long after you had left the beach. "I think you may be in love with an idea of a boy, rather than with an actual boy."

She did not take her hand away, allowing it to remain in her mother's clasp. "I don't think I am."

"But you don't know yet whether James sees you in the same way that you see him. That's the problem. And it might not be a good idea to allow yourself to love somebody you don't see very much and who may not feel the way you feel. It's just likely to make you miserable, I'd have thought."

Amanda pressed Clover's hand. She had never spoken to her with this degree of intimacy, and it felt to her as if she had been admitted to a whole new dimension of her daughter's life. It was like coming across one's child in some private moment and seeing the child, perhaps for the first time, as a person who was quite distinct from you, with a moral life of his or her own. Perhaps that was a transition that every parent experienced as a son or daughter moved from being an extension of the parent to having a life led separately from the parent, with its own tides of feeling, its own plans.

"Darling," she said, "there's an expression that people bandy about: love hurts. It sounds like one of those things that people say without thinking because they've read about it somewhere, or heard it in a song. But those things are often true, even if they sound corny and over-used. Love really does hurt. It hurts when you realise how much you love somebody. It hurts whether or not that person loves you back and everything goes well, or whether they don't and they ignore you or treat you badly. It just hurts, because that's the way love works. Does any of this make any sense to you?"

There was a murmur – nothing more.

"So as you go through life, you work out a way of dealing with it – just as you work out a way of dealing with the other things that happen to you. You could deny your feelings and try never to fall in love – lots of people do that – but that's no way to live. So you work out how to control the impact of love. You learn to protect yourself from being too badly bruised by it. You let yourself go, but always remembering that you have to keep part of you from being … well, I suppose, from being too badly hurt – from being drowned."

Clover looked away. "I like James. That's all."

"That's all?"

"Yes."

Amanda looked at her watch. "We need to begin our picnic. Perhaps you could go and fetch your brother from the water."

"He'll come if you shout *food*," said Clover. "Like a dog." She paused. "Do you think boys are a bit like dogs?"

Amanda laughed. "In some respects," she said.

20

They welcomed Amanda at the tennis club as if her absence had been three months rather than three years. Although there was a floating population of expatriates – those who came for a few years before going on somewhere else, or returning to the place they had come from – there were others who stayed for years, for the greater part of a lifetime in some cases. These people might spend much of their time elsewhere but seemed drawn back to the sheltering skirts of the place that having asked so little from them in terms of tax, then made no demands of them other than that they pay their bills and refrain from challenging corrupt politicians or well-connected developers. If they had the bad taste to be rich, then they might at least have the good taste to keep a low profile politically, and certainly not give others their advice.

With money, there came an ability to escape the normal constraints of geography. Most people did not have much choice about where they lived, and they stayed there year upon year. By contrast, the wealthy could move about as they wished, following the tides of whim and fashion. But too much absence could be a bad thing: being *off island* meant that you were away, but would probably return when you had had enough of the grind of existence in London or New York or wherever it was that you had gone to.

So the secretary of the tennis club merely added Amanda's name to the club competition ladder and sent her the bill for a renewed membership even without asking her whether she still wanted to play tennis.

"I heard you were back," she said when Amanda first visited the club. "I took the liberty of adding you to the doubles ladder:

we needed another woman for the mixed doubles and I thought of you."

Amanda had not objected. "My tennis is rusty," she said. "I joined a club in Edinburgh but you know how it is in Scotland. They have all-weather courts but that doesn't really help all that much if there's wind."

"You can book the pro."

"I will."

Clover went with her mother for her first lesson, and watched as Amanda returned serve after serve and responded to shouted instructions.

"He shouldn't shout at you like that," she muttered at the end of the lesson. "You're paying him, aren't you?"

"That's the whole point, darling. This island is full of people ..." – she almost said rich people, but stopped herself – "who pay others to shout at them. Personal trainers, and so on. There are hundreds of them."

Clover did not come to watch the second lesson, which took place the next afternoon, in that crucial hour before evening fell when the temperature was right for activities that involved exertion. The coach was impressed with the progress they had made and shouted less; her backhand, he said, was improving and would obviously get stronger with practice. At the end of the lesson, she made arrangements for the next session and then went into the club house for a shower. She did not intend to stay, as David would be back for dinner in an hour or so and she had nothing prepared, but she stopped by the noticeboard to look at the latest postings. The ladder was there – she saw her name in the mixed doubles section – and there was a poster advertising an exhibition match between the top-ranked player in Florida and a finalist from the Australian Open. It was to be on Boxing Day and there would be a dinner afterwards in aid of club funds. There was an appeal for a lost racquet – "of purely sentimental value" – removed accidentally, of course, from a car. No questions would be asked if the racquet were to be returned.

There was a voice behind her – so close that it startled her.

"See – there *is* a crime wave, whatever the Commissioner of Police may say."

She turned round to see George Collins. He was dressed for work, in a smart white shirt with buttoned-down collar and a red tie with a worked-in motif – a rod of Asclepius, the snake twirled round the physician's staff. In the confusion of the moment, her eye was drawn to the tie; he noticed, and smiled.

"People sometimes misunderstand this," he said. "One of my patients even asked if I was a snake-handler. I think she was disappointed when I explained that it all just had to do with an old Greek god."

She looked up at him, and she felt a sudden emptiness in her stomach. She had imagined that she would meet him on this trip; the island was too small for people to avoid one another. That could be done, of course, at the cost of some effort; two warring *grandes dames* who had left Palm Beach precisely to avoid contact with each other and had, by coincidence, both chosen Grand Cayman as their refuge, had been obliged to work out an unspoken rota that allowed them to frequent the same parties, but at different times; one came early and left early; the other arrived once the coast was clear.

She had thought it would be at a party, when she would have time to prepare herself. She had rehearsed in her mind how she would behave; how she would appear unfazed by the meeting;

how she would indicate by a casual, friendly demeanour that she bore no resentment or disappointment; that whatever had happened was a long time ago – three years was sufficient for people to get over most things, she felt, except, perhaps, sexual involvement: that was more difficult – the memory of intimacy was always there in the background, no matter how casually treated; the other had been admitted to the personal realm as others, acquaintances, friends, colleagues, had not.

But none of the scripts she had prepared came to her in this setting, before the tennis club noticeboard, where the opening remark had been about crime and a missing tennis racquet.

Banality came to her rescue. "Sometimes I wish somebody would steal my racquet," she said. "My game might improve with a new one."

He laughed. "I saw that you were having a lesson. I'm beyond all professional help, I'm afraid."

He looked at her, as if expecting her to comment on his tennis – she had never seen him play – but she said nothing. He waited, before continuing: "I thought you were never going to return."

She looked askance. "Why shouldn't I?"

"I just made the assumption."

"Well, you were wrong. Here I am."

He nodded. "You have the kids with you – so I assume it won't be for long."

She confirmed it would be for the duration of the school holidays and then she would return to Scotland, but only for a short while. "I'm coming back more permanently. Billy's going back to the Prep."

She saw that he seemed pleased to hear this news, and she became guarded. "I don't think that we should ..."

He interrupted her. "Should what? Talk to one another?"

"I didn't say that. But I don't think it would be wise, after what happened, for us to be seen together too often."

Again he queried her. "What counts as too often in this place? Once a month? Once a year?"

She spelled it out. "Too often means ever. I suppose I'd say that we shouldn't really see one another at all."

He raised his voice in protest, causing her to glance anxiously down the veranda; they were still by themselves. There was a note of frustration in his voice now. "I don't see what harm there is in two friends occasionally seeing one another."

"George," she said, "there's such a thing as disingenuousness. We can't pretend that we didn't, well, fall for one another."

He looked away, as if it was painful to be reminded.

"We can't pretend," she went on, "that people don't know that our marriages suffered as a result: you know what this place is like for gossip. We happen to live in a village of married couples. There are the keepers, with all their money, and the kept – and I'm one of the kept – and there are lots of us; it's just the way it is."

He interrupted her. "I've never heard it described that way ..."

She ignored the interruption. "My marriage more or less came to an end and now I'm rekindling it. I don't want to go through a separation again – or, worse still, a divorce."

"Don't sell yourself short. You've got a mind. You're not one of these women with nothing in their heads but thoughts of their next cocktail party or shopping trip to Miami. You're not that at all."

"Maybe not, but the reality of the situation is that I have no career. David and I can get on. We have children, and one of them is still quite young."

He looked at her with a mixture of disappointment and pity. "So you've made your bed and you're going to lie in it."

"You could put it that way. I'm being realistic."

He stared at her mutely.

"I'm sorry," she said. "I was very anxious about meeting you again. And now I've upset you."

He looked away. "You're right, though. We can't, can we?"

"Not really."

"It would have been …"

"It would have been good for both of us, yes, but I don't think we can."

He took a step away, and lowered his voice. "Let me tell you something," he said. "For the last three years, there has not been a day – not a single day – in which I haven't thought about you. Not necessarily for long periods, but even just for a few seconds – a fleeting thought, you'd call it – in which you have been there, in my mind, and I have let you in, so to speak."

She wanted to say: *me too, me too*. But she remained silent. *Do not tell your love.*

"Sometimes," he went on, "when I've been driving to work in the car, doing something as mundane as that, I've thought of you and I've whispered your name, or called it out, even, as if in agony. Why should I do this? Why should you have got under my skin to such an extent that I behave in a way that my psychiatric colleagues would find interesting? In fact – and this may amuse you – I mentioned this – disguising details, of course – to a psychiatrist friend and he said to me, 'Oh, that's not all that unusual; that's how agony is released, by shouting out the name of the person or the thing that haunts the mind.' And he said, too, that it was a way in which we tempt Fate to bring down upon us the thing that we dread could happen – the disclosure of our secret. Shout it out and control it that way. That's how he explained it.

"But I didn't really care about the explanation; what moved me was the fact that I had found something that I didn't think could exist. And that thing – the thing that I found – was very simple. Most people know all about it and have never really doubted it because their lives have been such as to give them a glimpse of this thing that they were not sure about, which is love, of course: the sheer fact of feeling love for another, of finding the one person – the only person, it seems – who makes the world make sense. It's like discovering the map that you've been looking for all your life and have never been able to find – the map that makes sense of the journey."

"George ..."

"No, I don't expect you to love me back, because that doesn't always happen, does it? So I accept that this is the way it is to be."

"Can't we just somehow get over this? I wanted ..."

He brushed this aside; it seemed that he was determined to finish what he wanted to say. "I shall continue to do what I'm doing, which is to be a doctor sorting out people's minor medical problems most of the time and every so often, I suppose, being able to do something more important for them. And I shall do this in a place that I don't really like – a place that I think has a tainted notion at its heart – that money should be able to be stashed away without doing anything for the people who actually do the work to produce it. I'm stuck with all that because even in places like this there are poor people and people who are treated badly and who need help with their varicose veins and digestive